THE PALE HOUSE DEVIL

RICHARD KADREY

T0035858

TITAN BOOKS

The Pale House Devil
Print edition ISBN: 9781803363899
Signed edition ISBN: 9781803367798
E-book edition ISBN: 9781803363905

Published by Titan Books
A division of Titan Publishing Group Ltd
144 Southwark Street, London SE1 0UP
www.titanbooks.com

First edition: October 2023
10 9 8 7 6 5 4 3 2 1

This is a work of fiction. All of the characters, organizations, and events portrayed in this novel are either products of the author's imagination or are used fictitiously. Any resemblance to actual persons, living or dead (except for satirical purposes), is entirely coincidental.

© Richard Kadrey 2023

Richard Kadrey asserts the moral right to be identified as the author of this work.

No part of this publication may be reproduced, stored in a retrieval system, or transmitted, in any form or by any means without the prior written permission of the publisher, nor be otherwise circulated in any form of binding or cover other than that in which it is published and without a similar condition being imposed on the subsequent purchaser.

A CIP catalogue record for this title is available from the British Library.

Printed and bound by CPI Group (UK) Ltd, Croydon, CR0 4YY.

1

It was close to midnight in Manhattan and they were still waiting in the van. Ford, short and wiry, was behind the wheel, while Neuland—bulkier and a foot taller—slouched in his seat trying to keep his head from hitting the ceiling of the van. They were dressed all in black and had black balaclavas on their faces so that the only things visible were their eyes—and someone would have to look carefully to see them. They'd been parked at the edge of the alley since twilight and both men had long since grown bored. Still they waited, their rifles propped against their legs.

Their employer—Mr. Garrick—hadn't given them a description of their target, just the bare outline of what was supposed to happen and how they were supposed to stop it. It was annoying. They didn't work that way normally, but Garrick promised to pay them double their normal fee, so they went along with his nonsense.

"Do you think that's them?" said Neuland.

A few yards ahead of them in the alley, a well-dressed man and a haggard woman appeared to be negotiating some kind of deal. Ford watched through what resembled a pair of binoculars, but the tubes were carved from a yew tree and the lenses were the shaved corneas from the eyes of thirteen hanged men.

"It's not them," said Ford. "From the look of them, the girl's got pills or party potions and the guy's a tourist who doesn't know how to haggle. Besides, they're both dodos."

Dodo was what Ford occasionally—and many others routinely—called the undead. It bothered Neuland, who was also undead.

"Please don't use that word. It's demeaning," Neuland said. "And it makes you sound like a hick."

"Sorry."

"We prefer *Marcheur*."

"You're right. I'm tired and didn't think."

"It's all right."

"No. It was rude and I'm sorry."

"You can't help how you were raised."

"But you're my partner and I should be more considerate."

"Apology accepted," said Neuland. "Now, are we going to shoot either of those two or not?"

"No. The deal is supposed to be someone alive selling something to a Marcheur. That lets these two off the hook."

"Maybe. Let's keep an eye on them. One of them could still be involved."

The van felt cramped after all this time, and they'd finished the coffee hours ago. Ford wanted a smoke, but didn't dare light up where the cherry-red end of the cigarette could be spotted. So, they waited in silence.

The dealer and the tourist finished their business, and the tourist went into the rear of a bodega while the woman remained in the alley. She checked her watch several times.

"You're right," said Ford. "She's part of the deal."

"Nervous?"

"Impatient. I mean, look at her twitch. It won't be long now."

"I hope you're right."

They sat quietly for a few minutes before Ford said, "Really, man, I'm sorry about the dodo thing."

"I told you it's all right."

"Thank you."

"You're welcome, and also, you should look out the window. This might be it."

Ford sat up as a young woman approached the Marcheur. The woman was in a purple velvet dress and had straight black hair that hung down to her waist. He scanned the two women through his special binoculars.

"You're right," he said. "The one in the velvet dress is alive. But I don't like it."

"Me neither. Garrick didn't say the target was a woman. Just dressed in velvet, right?"

"That's right."

Neuland shook his head. "I don't shoot women."

Ford looked at him. "We've both shot women."

"Really evil ones. Like Elsbeth Bathory evil. Not some little thing in a party dress."

"Let's keep watching. Maybe she's the right kind for shooting."

For the first time, the nature of the assignment weighed down on Neuland. He didn't like the situation one bit, but he knew that if this was indeed their target, he'd have to take the shot. It was his job to kill the living. Ford killed the dead.

Neuland said, "Please tell me they're plotting something nefarious."

"Shit," said Ford. "Shit."

"What?" He didn't like the tone of Ford's voice.

"There's something else. The party dress?"

"Yes?"

"She's pregnant."

Neuland reached out and took the binoculars. The haggard undead woman's aura was a grayish purple while the young woman's was a bright purple.

"What the hell is this?" said Neuland. "If she's selling her kid, I sure as hell will shoot her."

"Yeah, Sir Galahad? And kill the kid too? I'm going to keep watching. I want to know exactly what's going on."

Neuland was mad now. He knew his distaste for shooting women was hypocritical since they were every bit as capable of evil as men. Worse, not wanting to shoot a mother was the rankest kind of sentimentality. He didn't like having strong emotional responses to these situations. Strong emotions were for the living, like Ford. He could fly into a rage at a moment's notice and it accomplished nothing. The undead were supposed to be above such things, but here he was. Fretting about some stranger selling what, rationally, was hers to sell.

Another moment passed and Ford said, "A necklace."

"Not the kid?"

"Not the kid."

"What kind of necklace?"

"Expensive looking. Earrings too. Some bracelets. All gold. All nice-looking stuff."

"Let me see," said Neuland, and Ford handed him the binoculars. He was right, the undead woman was examining a pile of jewelry in a decorated wooden box that the young woman held out.

Neuland handed the binoculars back to Ford and said, "You know what this means."

"Of course."

"It might cost us our fee."

"There's no helping that."

"I guess not."

Ford started the van and they drove to Mr. Garrick's office, where they'd arranged to meet after the hit. They let themselves into the building with a key Garrick had given them and rode the elevator to the penthouse level of the old office building. Neuland was out of the elevator first and didn't bother knocking on Garrick's office door before going in. Garrick, sixtyish and in a sharply tailored suit, looked up in surprise. He smiled at the men.

"That was quick," he said. "You boys are every bit as efficient as they say."

The two men came in and Neuland stood very close to Garrick's desk so he could loom over the man. They'd left their rifles in the van.

"Efficient," said Neuland. "That's because we can read a scene and know what's happening, even from a distance."

"It's what keeps me alive and my partner in one piece," said Ford.

"We read the scene tonight, Mr. Garrick."

"And we didn't like it."

Garrick scowled at the men. "What's it your business to like or not like a particular killing? I hired you to do a job. Did you do it or not?"

"No," said Ford.

"You see, the target was pregnant."

"What difference does that make?" said Garrick.

"She was selling her personal jewelry," said Ford. "It was in a silly little box. Something cheap and gaudy. The kind someone young like her would love."

"And?" said Garrick.

"It was very expensive jewelry," said Neuland. "Much too expensive for her, considering the quality of her dress. The jewelry might have been hers, but she didn't buy it."

"They were a gift," said Ford.

"From you," said Neuland.

Garrick sat back in his big leather office chair. "What the hell are you talking about? I hired you as killers, not psychics."

"There's nothing psychic about it," said Ford.

"It's like we said, about being able to read a scene. You see, a young woman selling jewelry like that—jewelry she couldn't possibly afford—can only mean one thing."

"And what's that?" said Garrick snidely.

"That she's using her rich lover's gifts to her to finance an escape," said Ford.

"From the lover," said Neuland. "You hired us to kill her because you got her pregnant, and that's an inconvenience. She was smart enough to know that something was up and was buying a ticket out of town."

Garrick slammed his hands on his desk and stood up. "Don't get high and mighty with me, boys. You're murderers. Not priests. And you don't get a cent until the bitch is dead."

Ford and Neuland looked at each other.

"I think you should explain it to him," said Ford.

"Obviously," said Neuland as he took a Sig Sauer P220 pistol from his jacket and emptied the entire clip of .45 rounds into Garrick's body. The man slammed to the floor, his blood splashing onto the desk and the curtains and the window behind him.

The moment his partner was finished, Ford began going through the drawers in Garrick's desk looking for money. Neuland went through Garrick's pockets.

"Anything?" said Ford.

Neuland shook his head.

"Two thousand in cash in his wallet, but that's it."

"Damn. Well, let's take it and go. We need to leave town."

"Not yet," said Neuland. "I don't think we're done. Garrick is the kind of guy to have an insurance policy."

Ford stopped.

"You're probably right."

"We'll know soon."

A minute passed before Garrick's corpse began to twitch. His limbs convulsed and his eyes fluttered open and shut. His shoulders spasmed and his teeth chattered as if he was cold. Then he stopped, grabbed his desk chair, and dragged himself to his feet. Erect, he looked at Ford and Neuland and said, "You're both dead men."

"No. I'm the dead one," said Neuland.

"And I kill the dead," said Ford, pulling his own pistol. He shot Garrick between the eyes with one of his special cold iron bullets and the man fell back to the floor.

The killers left, knowing he wouldn't get up again.

"So, where are we going?" said Neuland. "We can't stay in New York."

"Europe?"

"I don't like flying and I hate ships even more."

"We could drive to Montreal. Bigsby is always offering us jobs," said Ford.

"Too cold. My joints get stiff."

Ford said, "Right. So where?"

Neuland thought for a moment.

"West. As far west as we can go."

"Like cowboys."

"Sure. Like cowboys."

"Goddamn Garrick," said Ford.

"Lousy dodo," said Neuland.

Ford looked at him. Neuland laughed, then so did Ford. He said, "I'll get us train tickets."

2

They caught a train the next morning from the Port Authority for a three-day trip to Los Angeles. Ford got them a sleeper cabin and they settled in. During the night they'd bought some paperback mystery novels and magazines. Each man had earbuds and music on their phones. They both enjoyed trains and understood how to travel by land—how to slow their pace, how to move within the confines of their small cabin and be comfortable with longs periods of quiet with just the rattle of the tracks filling the space between them.

Ford had picked up snacks the night before, but around six he decided to get a real dinner in the dining car and asked if Neuland wanted to join him.

"No thanks. Those places make me uncomfortable."

Ford said, "Yeah, but we should really talk about our work situation. And I'm starving."

"Can't we talk when you get back?"

"I'd like someone to watch my back on the off chance that Garrick has friends. Besides, I'm probably going to fall asleep when I get back."

It was the nature of the undead not to sleep. Neuland would

simply go into a dreamless fugue state for a few hours every couple of days and that was all the rest he needed. Sleep was one of the few things for which he envied the living, and he didn't want to deprive his partner of a pleasure he wished for himself.

"Fine," he said, suddenly annoyed by their situation. About being on the run. However, there was nothing to do but go along with it and see how it played out. He put on his shoes and followed Ford to the dining car.

Inside, they found a table by a window. They were in deep country and there was nothing but hills and greenery as far as either of them could see.

"I wish I knew about trees and that kind of thing," said Ford.

"Why?"

"Then I'd know what we were looking at instead of it being just a big mishmash of..." He waved his hands at the window.

"Stuff," said Neuland. "Random nature stuff."

"Exactly. Random nature stuff."

"It's the price of growing up a city kid."

Ford said, "I should have bought a book on trees before we left New York."

"You can get one in LA."

"Speaking of LA..."

"Yes. Everyone will know what happened in New York," said Neuland. "Do you think there will be guns waiting for us?"

"It's true that they'll know, but I don't know anyone in LA who's particularly fond of Garrick. Do you?"

"No. But the local outfits might object to the overall nature of our actions."

"If no one will give us work, then we'll move on," said Ford.

"San Francisco?"

"Everybody loves us in San Francisco."

"But let's check out LA first," said Neuland. "Get a feel for where our reputation stands. If we need to, maybe take a job or two at a reduced rate. Just to show we're team players."

Ford was eating a steak with green beans and mashed potatoes. Neuland hadn't eaten in years, but he appreciated the smell of it even if the sight of the living shoveling food into their mouths was unpleasant. He didn't order any food, but had a cup of black coffee in front of him just to fit in. Every now and then he took small sips, knowing he'd vomit it all up when they got back to the cabin.

"I was thinking the same thing," said Ford. "Play it cool. Get the lay of the land. Besides, we haven't been in LA in years. Maybe we can take in the sights."

Neuland took a sip of his coffee and said, "I'm going back to the cabin. That guy keeps looking at me funny."

"A cop?" said Ford, concern in his voice.

"I don't know, but I don't like it. Besides, I want to get this stuff out of my stomach. I'll see you back there."

"Okay. I won't be long. Just try to relax. We're both a little on edge after last night."

Neuland nodded and left the dining car.

Back in the cabin, he vomited easily into the toilet and flushed the coffee away. Sitting on his bunk, he took a big gulp from a bottle of goofer juice, the only thing he consumed. It was a combination of blood, holy water, soil from a grave in consecrated ground, and a dozen other ingredients that the brewers held secret. The juice kept Neuland sharp, so he could do his job well, and not become his greatest fear—just another shambling pile of undead bones, as useless as a skid row wino.

Ford came back to the cabin a few minutes later, kicked off his shoes, and settled into his bunk. He said, "You feeling any better?"

"About what?"

"Getting out of the dining car. I checked around before I came back. The crowd looked like the usual bored dummies to me."

"Good. Maybe I was just a little paranoid."

"It'll be good to have a couple of days to unwind."

"It might be nice to go to the beach when we get to LA," said Neuland. "I haven't seen the ocean in years."

"I'd like that. The beach. Let's do that."

Ford settled back in his bunk with a camera magazine and read about the new models coming out. Neuland read a Patricia Highsmith novel.

Around ten, there was a light knock on their door. The two men looked at each other. Neuland got up and said, "Who is it?"

"A friend with a business proposition."

It was a man's voice, low and rumbling.

Neuland looked back at Ford, who shook his head. "We're on vacation," said Neuland. "You must be looking for someone else."

The voice came again. "Only if there's another dead man on this train."

Neuland opened the door and a man pushed past him into the small cabin. Though his voice had been deep and large through the door, he wasn't that big. He wore a wrinkled suit jacket and his thin hair was a mess. Someone who didn't know how to travel well, thought Neuland. Still, the man had something going for him. He knew what Neuland was.

The stranger spoke again. "My name is Jake Wetton. I'm a private investigator from Pasadena and I know one of you is a dodo." He looked at Neuland. "You, to be exact."

"What do you want, Jake Wetton, P-fucking-I?" said Ford.

"I'll tell you, but first you both need to know that I called my partner and told him about what I'm doing. If anything happens to me, he'll alert the authorities who deal with *things* like your friend."

"You didn't answer my question."

Jake looked from one man to the other and laughed. "Money, you asshole. Cash now or my partner calls the garbage squad. You have three minutes to hand it over."

"How much do you want?" said Neuland.

"All of it. Everything you have." He looked at Neuland. "Something like you, what do you need money for? If you have money it means you took it from a living person. Someone who deserved it."

"What about me?" said Ford. "I'm alive."

"True, but fuck you for throwing in with a goddamn ghoul. Now show me some cash. You have about two minutes left."

"Two minutes," said Neuland.

Ford shook his head. "That's not very long."

"Damn right," said Wetton. "Now let's see it."

Ford stood from his bunk. He said, "Let me make a counteroffer," and punched Wetton in the jaw. The man dropped to his knees, blood streaming from a split lip. Ford hit him again and knocked the man unconscious. Neuland got his bottle of goofer juice and poured some into Wetton's mouth. The man sputtered but kept it down. He came to a moment later and pulled himself up from the floor.

"That was a big mistake," he said. "You're both fucked now."

"I don't think so," said Ford.

Neuland held out his phone. "No bars," he said.

"No bars on mine either," said Ford. "And it's been that way most of the day."

"So, you were lying. You didn't call anyone."

Wetton wobbled on his feet. He wiped at his bleeding mouth with the sleeve of his jacket, then made a face and spit on the floor.

"Got a funny taste in your mouth?" said Ford. "It's called goofer juice."

Wetton went pale. "You didn't."

"He didn't," said Neuland. "I did. You might want to go lie down. You have about twelve hours before it takes effect."

"Until you die," said Ford. "And then wake up."

"And are like me," said Neuland.

Wetton slumped against the wall. "You're lying."

"Wait and see."

"I'm a ghoul," whispered Wetton.

"Not yet. But soon."

He looked at Neuland. "Filthy baby eater."

Ford laughed and said, "Yeah. Babies. Cats and dogs, too."

"And PIs," said Neuland. "You can't help the hunger. It grows and grows. Don't worry. It's not your fault. You're just another *thing* now."

"Oh god," said Wetton. "Mother Mary."

He pushed his way out of the cabin, tripped and fell in the corridor that ran the length of the train car. "Mother Mary protect me," he said, and stumbled back toward the dining car.

Neuland shut the cabin door. "Do you think we should go after him?"

Ford lay back on his cot. "You heard him. A nice Catholic boy like that. He'll do the right thing."

Neuland sat and slowly said, "Baby eater."

Ford gave him a sympathetic look. "The shit some people will believe."

Neuland got up and went into the little bathroom to throw water on his face, still weighing whether he should go after Wetton and finish him. But a moment later came the sound of a muffled explosion. He went out and looked at his partner. Even on a noisy train, both men recognized the sound of a gunshot.

Ford smiled. "What did I tell you? He handled it himself."

"Idiot," said Neuland.

"Completely."

"One more reason I'm glad we're heading west."

"You mean how there are too many second-rate randos with big ideas back home?" said Ford.

"Big ideas and big guns. I need to get away from it for a while."

"Sounds good to me."

Neuland wiped his face on a towel and scowled as something occurred to him. He went to his bunk and said, "What if he had a satellite phone? He might have called his partner after all."

Ford thought about it. "He was a mess. Small time. A guy like that doesn't have a satellite phone."

"Maybe he's a gadget freak like some people." Neuland nodded toward Ford's camera magazine. "I should have followed him to his cabin to be sure."

"If he had a satellite phone he would have said so. It's going to be all right."

"Maybe," said Neuland.

Both men sat up the rest of the night with their guns nearby. Eventually the train stopped, and they heard the sound of police in the car examining Wetton's room and removing the body. No one came to their cabin. In the morning, Ford went to the dining car, ate a quick breakfast, and came back. Neuland was still waiting with his pistol handy.

Ford lay down on his bunk and said, "Relax. It's over."

Neuland put his gun under his pillow and lay down too.

Wetton reminded him of the men—it was always men and mostly from the city—who would come to the swamp where he'd spent so many years in servitude. The men all wanted the same thing: secrets. Secrets to power. Secrets to riches. Secrets to immortality. They would offer mansions, exotic cars, women— even children. Whatever they thought of as valuable. But the swamp people could spot a card shark or thief as easily as a buzzard spots a carrion meal. The lucky strangers got away with their lives, but often missing an eye or some fingers because there was powerful magic in those things. The unlucky men joined Neuland in his numb servitude. He never felt sorry for a single one of them.

Ford slept and Neuland willed himself into a fugue state, but neither man really rested. Both awoke bitter that what was supposed to have been a pleasant trip had been completely spoiled.

3

I t walked through the parlor of the old house, though few would consider what it did truly walking. It oozed on its belly and dragged the rest of itself on many short legs, like some huge, gelatinous insect. The tube of its mouth—lined with both teeth and slits, like that of a baleen whale—protruded as it moved, sucking mice and spiders into its enormous belly. It even lapped dust with its long tongue because it could sustain itself on mere filth. No one could see it unless it wanted to be seen, but there had been few enough people in the house over the last few years for it to remember the pleasure of showing its form. So, it remained in a state of ghostly transparency, its presence marked only by its tiny footprints on the dirty floor and the fact that the house remained virtually vermin free even though it had been empty for many years. Few things outside dared to come in, and nothing caught inside ever got out.

Still, it wasn't content.

It longed for more stimulation and better food. It slept for months at a time, so that seasons seemed to pass by in a single day. It remembered when people used to live in the house, and how fun it had been to play with them because they were so soft and pink and tasty. It would appear before them and then disappear a moment later. There were shrieks. Wide-eyed sprints down dark halls before they tumbled down the stairs. The crunch of their bones. It missed the smell and the taste of humanity. But here it was, trapped like a roach within the house's whitewashed walls. It would have wept if it had eyes. Properly moaned if it could. The best it could muster in its sorrow was a slurping, gurgling trill through its long-tubed mouth that reminded it of the moans of the screaming handyman it had once drowned in the upstairs tub.

So, it waited, in boredom and misery. The only thing that sustained it was knowing its anguish wouldn't last forever. This was a house, and it knew the soft things didn't let go of houses easily. Sooner or later, someone would come back. Sooner or later, someone would return to play.

4

There was no ambush waiting for them in LA, but there wasn't any work either. Everybody knew about the Garrick affair and no one liked it.

During their first couple of days in town, Ford and Neuland set up meetings with Jimmy Graham, Big Tommy Wong, and Mia Solonotsyn. They even rented a car and drove out to Covina to see Rudy Jay, with his greasy hair, his bad breath, and his too-small suits. They played it cool because being cool was their nature, even when in dire circumstances—which the trip was turning out to be. Every contact they had, every lowlife who'd ever approached them with a job offer, now had the same answer: "Fuck off."

The crews didn't want to work with Neuland especially. Some intrepid reporter had stumbled on evidence of LAPD's Marcheur clean-up squad. Rumors of the undead walking among the living were all over the local media and no crew wanted to stick its neck out. Especially for a couple of killers who'd murdered their own client and then split town.

"We are shit out of luck in LA," said Ford back in their suite at the Hollywood Roosevelt Hotel.

Neuland sat on one of the beds with the TV remote in his hand. An old black-and-white cowboy movie he didn't recognize played silently on the set.

"It's mostly my fault," Neuland said. "I'm the pariah right now. Maybe you should go out on your own. At least for a while. I can go to Mexico and maybe the story about the undead will play itself out."

Ford dropped into a leather chair by the window. "You're not going anywhere. We're partners. And what we do doesn't work without both of us."

"You could split town. Find a new dead man—or woman—to partner with."

"Stop talking like that. You sound like my grandma. Anything bad happened, it was the end of the world. This is just a rough patch. We'll get through it."

Neuland stared at the TV for a moment. During a commercial he said, "I'm not sorry about New York. If I had to do it all over again, I would."

"Me too, so stop obsessing and let's think this through."

"I don't think there's a lot to think about. You said it. We're done in LA."

Ford got out his phone and scanned his address book. He said, "What about showbiz creeps? I still have some producer and agent contacts. There's always a shitty movie in trouble somewhere with a leading man the studio wants to murder for the insurance."

"Maybe," said Neuland, brightening. "It's better than nothing, I suppose. Sure. Make some calls."

Ford made some calls. A dozen of them. Neuland went out to get him a burrito from his favorite place a few blocks away. The round trip took perhaps thirty minutes. When he returned, he found Ford standing in the open door of a fire exit, puffing a cigarette and blowing the smoke into the empty stairwell. Ford thanked Neuland for the burrito, but just held it to his side.

Neuland said, "How did it go?"

Ford flicked his cigarette butt down the metal stairs. He said, "We are shit out of luck in LA."

They checked out of the hotel the next morning and drove north in the rental car, finally ditching it at Oakland Airport. Ford had used a fake ID to rent it, so there was no way to trace it back to them.

In San Francisco, they decided not to set up meets. Coming at the problem head-on hadn't worked in LA, so it was time to try a new strategy. Instead of begging for work, they simply appeared in certain bars and restaurants in North Beach, Chinatown, the Mission, and SoMa. They made sure it was known they were around, but they didn't make a big deal of it. They knew word would soon circulate to the right people. Work would come their way. It had to. If no one wanted them in San Francisco it meant heading to Europe, and Ford dreaded a long flight with Neuland white-knuckling it the whole way. Though he couldn't really blame him. Neuland didn't like talking about his past, but one thing he'd revealed was that he'd died in a plane crash somewhere down south, somewhere people were comfortable with the old ways of doing things. Working with spirits, bones, and potions. At the crash site, he'd been one of the lucky ones intact enough to have his body stolen and then brought back to something like life. Neuland said he'd spent years killing and stealing to work off his life debt. Ford didn't know Neuland's exact age, but he was certain the man had a couple of lifetimes on him. No, for both their sakes, San Francisco had to pay off.

5

On their fourth afternoon in the city, there was a knock on the door of their hotel room. Neuland went to see who it was, and since they weren't expecting anyone, Ford sat on the sofa with his pistol hidden by his leg.

When he opened the door, Neuland found a small blonde woman in an expensive business suit. She appeared to be in her early twenties and was very pretty, but he was more interested in the fact that, while her suit fit well, she didn't seem entirely comfortable in it. She was trying to look commanding and in charge but was a bit embarrassed by it.

"Who are you?" Neuland said.

"Tilda Rosenbloom," she said quietly.

Neuland didn't recognize the name, so he didn't let her in. "Who sent you?"

"No one. I just heard they were around."

"From who?"

"Jesus Cortazar. At the Black Heart last night."

The Black Heart was a biker bar on Valencia Street that the men liked because, even though their dark suits stood out among all the leather, the patrons of the bar were too smart to bother them.

Neuland took a step back and let the woman inside. When he closed the door, she jumped a little. He went to join Ford on the sofa, but Tilda was too nervous to sit. She stood in the center of the room like she might bolt out the door at any minute.

Ford said, "Cortazar told us he didn't want to do business. Did he change his mind?"

Tilda shook her head. "No. This is for someone else."

"So, someone *did* send you."

"I mean, not to you specifically. Just to someone like you."

"And who was it that sent you in the general direction of people like us?"

Tilda reached into her shoulder bag, took out $20,000 in hundred-dollar bills, and handed them to Ford. He and Neuland looked over the money.

Neuland set his hand with the money on his knee. "This isn't killing money," he said. "This is stern-talking-to money."

Tilda took gave them another $10,000 from her purse.

Ford said, "That's closer, but still..."

"Who's the job for?" said Neuland.

Tilda closed her purse and looked down nervously at her expensive shoes. "You don't know him. He's not usually involved in this sort of thing."

"And you are?"

She shook her head like she was both frightened and a little ashamed.

"You don't have to be scared of us."

"I just haven't met men like you before."

"What? A couple of guys who want to go to the beach?" said Ford.

Neuland said, "I haven't seen the ocean in years."

Tilda half-smiled and looked away. "Now you're making fun of me."

"No, we're not. We're going to the beach later. Want to come along? We can talk business by the water."

She looked scared again, but Ford raised his eyebrows comically high and after a moment she smiled but didn't say anything.

"Let's try this," said Neuland. "Are you paying us for a job, or did someone give you the money to hire us?"

"The second thing."

"Who gave you the money?"

"My boss."

"And who's that?"

"Shepherd Mansfield."

The men exchanged puzzled looks. Neuland shrugged. "We haven't heard of him."

Tilda nodded. "He doesn't really consort with you kind of people." She stopped and her eyes went a little wide as if she scared herself. "Oh my god. That sounded very judgmental."

Ford held up his hand. "It's okay. So, he's not a crook. What is he?"

"Afraid."

"Of who?"

"He says he thinks something is after him."

"Thinks or knows?"

Neuland said, "Why did you say some*thing* and not some*one*?"

"I'm not sure. I'm just telling you what he told me."

"And he wants us to..." Neuland didn't say *kill* because he knew it would scare her all over again. "...remove this thing from his life?"

"Yes."

The men whispered to each other.

Neuland said, "It's not bad money, considering no one is exactly beating down our door."

"You're right. Still, I don't like it. The Garrick thing was a weird setup and look how that turned out."

"Yes, but she's offering us thirty thousand up front. We take it and if we don't like the job, we tell Mansfield that we're keeping it for wasting our time."

"If she's walking around with thirty K in her purse, Mansfield can afford more."

"Definitely."

Neuland turned to Tilda and said, "If we take the job, we'll need another $20,000."

She said, "That's fine," without hesitation.

The men nodded.

Ford said, "When does he want us?"

"As soon as possible."

"Well, we're not leaving today."

"We still haven't seen the ocean," said Neuland.

"Would you like to come with us, Tilda?"

She bit her lip nervously, but she no longer looked like she was going to bolt from the room. The men smiled and she gave them a little smile back.

"I don't know."

Ford said, "If you're worried about your boss, we won't tell."

Neuland crossed his heart and held up his right hand as if making a pledge. "Honest."

Tilda twisted the toe of one shoe into the soft carpet. "You're not at all what I thought you'd be like."

"What did you think we'd be like?"

"Scarier."

"You were scared before," said Ford. "You're not scared now?"

"A little. But not like before."

"Then you'll come with us?"

She took a deep breath and let it out. Bounced once on her heels and shook her head as if she couldn't believe what she was about to say. "Sure."

Neuland called for a car to pick them up. They went downstairs to the front of the hotel and in a little while a long black limo drove up. The driver held the door open for them, which made Tilda laugh. Inside, she said she'd never been in a limo before.

There was liquor in the side compartment.

"Then let's drink to your first ride," said Ford. He poured two shots and handed her one.

She looked at Neuland. "Aren't you going to have a drink?"

He took out his goofer juice. "I have my own."

They all clinked glasses and drank.

They sipped whiskey on the way to the beach and Tilda played with all the buttons on the console, opening windows, turning on the lights and the TV in the side panel opposite the liquor cabinet. She laughed, no longer sounding scared.

The limo went to Ocean Beach and they walked along the sand, just out of reach of the lapping tide. There was a small carnival on the edge of Golden Gate Park across the street, so they walked over and Ford bought cotton candy for Tilda and himself. Neuland took little sips from his bottle.

Tilda said to him, "You're not eating and you keeping drinking that stuff. Are you sick?"

"No. I just prefer this to cotton candy."

"Is it moonshine? Can I try?"

"It's not good for you."

"Please."

He handed her the bottle. She took off the cork, sniffed the contents, and sneezed violently. "Man, that's way too strong for me."

She handed back the bottle and the men laughed. Neuland said, "It's an acquired taste."

Tilda laughed too and looked at him for a minute. Then she looked back at Ford. She looped her arms in each of theirs as they strolled down the long walkway at the edge of the beach.

"What's it like?" she said.

"What we do for a living?" said Ford.

"Yes."

He shrugged. "Like anything else, I suppose. You do a good job. You do it as fast as you can and you don't leave loose ends. You do all that, and you have an employer who wants more of your services."

"It's that simple taking a life?"

"We don't take just any life," said Neuland. "They're special people."

She looked at him for a moment. "Like bad people?"

"Exactly."

Tilda shook her head and smiled. "It's a whole new world to me. I've never even held a gun."

"Would you like to?"

She looked at Neuland again. "Now?"

"Sure. I know a place."

"At the beach?"

"The old Sutro Baths up ahead. Do you know them?"

"I've seen them from the road, but I've never gone down to check them out."

"See? Hardly anyone ever goes down there at this time of day."

Tilda didn't say anything for a minute.

Ford said, "Look out at the ocean. Fog is rolling in. We'll be practically invisible."

"Won't they hear us shooting?"

"I have a silencer. With the noise of the waves, no one will hear a thing."

Tilda looked from Ford to Neuland. She laughed. "Oh my god."

"That sounded like a yes to me," Neuland said.

"Was that a yes?" said Ford.

Tilda didn't speak, but shook her head minutely.

They walked up the hill to the long set of stairs that led down to the ruins of the old baths. By the time they got there, fog was rolling in over the most distant rocks.

It was another long stroll to where the walkway came to an abrupt end. On the right was a deep cave where water splashed somewhere inside. To the left was the ocean and the concrete bones of the old baths.

They came to a stop, and Tilda leaned on a rusted guardrail over stones where the water pooled. The fog was moving in fast now, blotting out the beach and much of the ocean. "The end of the world," she said.

"No better place to learn to shoot," said Ford. He took his pistol from his jacket, screwed on the silencer, and handed it to her.

Tilda weighed the gun in her hand. "It's heavy," she said after a while.

"Don't worry about that. It's just a little 9mm walking-around gun. The weight will help keep it from bouncing back and smacking you in the head."

Tilda stared at the pistol for a moment, then out at the fog. It surrounded them on all sides. She put her arm out and pointed it at what she could see of the Pacific. "Like this?" she said.

Neuland stood behind her, had her hold the pistol with both hands, and adjusted her stance.

"Now?" said Tilda.

"Now."

"I'm scared."

"You're walking into unknown territory. It's smart to be scared," said Ford. "Just don't let it stop you."

There was a moment of silence, then three quick *pop-pop-pops*. Tilda lowered her arms and put a hand over her mouth. "Was that me?"

"That was you," said Ford.

"It was... easy."

"Fun?" said Neuland.

"I think so."

"Try it again. Do you remember the stance?"

"Like this?"

"Perfect."

There were three more quick *pops*. Tilda held up her arms and whooped into the fog. When she realized what she'd done, she covered her mouth and laughed. "I'm sorry. I don't usually do that."

Ford took the pistol from her and unscrewed the silencer. "You're a regular cowgirl now. You get to whoop it up."

Tilda started to whoop again, but caught herself and shook her head. She said, "Can we go back to the car now?"

"Are you okay?" said Neuland.

She nodded. "The fog is just cold. That's probably why my hands are shaking a little. I'd really like another drink."

Tilda shivered as they went back to the limo. Ford took off his jacket and put it around her. When they got to the car, the driver held the door for them again.

They settled in, and this time Tilda poured drinks for herself and Ford. She gestured for Neuland to join them. He took out his bottle and they all drank together.

It was rush hour and traffic was heavy getting back to their hotel, so the limo was forced to stop frequently. During one stop, Tilda gave both Ford and Neuland a peck on the cheek.

"Thank you," she said, a little tipsy.

"For showing you how to shoot?" said Ford.

She shook her head. "Partly. But mostly for taking me seriously enough to ask."

They raised their drinks and toasted each other.

They drank all the way back to the hotel and Tilda fell asleep on the sofa in their suite. Neuland took an extra blanket from the closet and put it over her.

"Nice kid," said Ford.

"I don't think she gets out much."

"Me neither. You think she's small-town, or someone's got a leash on her?"

"I guess we'll know when we meet Mansfield."

Later, each of them went to their bedrooms. They left the $30,000 on the coffee table knowing it would be all right there.

6

I n the morning, they checked out of the hotel and drove north in a Silver Cloud Rolls-Royce that Mansfield had loaned Tilda for the trip. They were heading for Redding at the northern tip of California. The Rolls was a large, very expensive car and she didn't seem entirely comfortable driving it. Ford and Neuland knew the car was there to impress them with Mansfield's wealth, and it did. They upped their demand from $20,000 to finish the job to $30,000.

Tilda just grinned and steered them across the Golden Gate Bridge into Marin. "I doubt another $10,000 will bother Mr. Mansfield," she said. "The feeling I get is that if you do the job fast, he's ready to give you the money, the car, me, and a trip to the moon if you want it."

"He has a lot of friends on the moon, does he?" said Ford.

Neuland sat next to Tilda up front. Ford was sprawled out in the back.

"Mr. Mansfield has friends everywhere. He's had all kinds of people over to the house. Politicians. Businessmen. Even sheiks."

"But no moon men?" said Neuland.

Tilda shook her head and smiled at Neuland. "No moon men."

"Maybe we'll be his moon men. Weirdos from another world."

"Speak for yourself," said Ford. "I'm from Brooklyn."

Tilda said, "I want to go to New York someday."

"It's the best city in the world."

"London is nice," said Neuland.

"Yeah, nice. New York is magic."

"I'd love to see it."

"When this is over, we'll show it to you sometime," Ford said.

Tilda looked at him in the rearview mirror. "Really?"

Neuland said, "We know the best places."

"But give it a few weeks. We have to smooth some feathers back there before we can go back full-time."

"Oh," said Tilda, her voice going a little cold. "Sure."

"You think we're lying," said Neuland. "Teasing you about New York and then brushing you off."

"People don't do nice things like that for me. Take me places and show me new things."

Ford put his head up between them. "What do people do for you?"

"Nothing. Mr. Mansfield keeps me pretty busy."

"No boyfriends or girlfriends?"

"A couple. Boyfriends, that is. But they always went away. Either I was too busy, or Mr. Mansfield scared them."

"He sounds like a great guy," said Neuland.

"I'm in love already," said Ford. "Tell us more about him."

Tilda sighed. "He's in his eighties. He hardly eats or sleeps. When he does sleep, he has terrible nightmares."

Neuland said, "What kind?"

"I don't know. He won't talk about them."

"Keep going," said Ford.

"Most of the time he's in a wheelchair and he's horrible about it," said Tilda. "Always yelling and throwing things. Sometimes he's just on a cane or two. He's a little better then, but not much."

"He must pay you a lot if he has the right to throw things at you," said Neuland.

"He pays me well. And anyway, he's family. My great-grandfather."

Ford said, "How does he make his money?"

"He took over the family's companies when grandpa and my dad died. They—we—have interests in logging, shipping, construction. And those are just the companies I know about. I'm sure there are other things he doesn't talk about."

"Why would he hide things from his great-granddaughter? It seems like you have a right to know about the family's finances."

"Not according to Mr. Mansfield."

"Do you always call him Mr. Mansfield?" said Neuland. "I mean, you're family. That's a little formal."

"It's what I call him when it's something to do with business. The rest of time he's Papa Shep. The thing is, these last few years, all there's been is business. So, Mr. Mansfield is a habit now."

"Should we start calling ourselves 'Mister'?" said Ford.

"Mr. Neuland and Mr. Ford."

Ford made a face. "Makes us sounds like bankers."

"Or insurance salesmen."

"Let's forget 'Mister.'"

Neuland checked his watch. "It's only two hundred miles to Redding. We should be there early evening."

"Yeah," said Tilda, a note of uncertainty in her voice. "That's something I wasn't supposed to tell you until we were on the road."

"What's that?" said Ford.

"We're not going all the way to Redding today."

"Why the hell not?"

"We're staying in a little town called Williams tonight. It's about halfway there. The trip is going to take three days."

"This is Mansfield's idea?" said Neuland.

"Yes."

"Why only halfway?"

"He said that if we went there too quickly, whoever was watching him might know something was going on and maybe do something. This way, if we go slowly, it won't suspect a thing."

"Today you said 'whoever,' like it's a person, but yesterday you said 'something.' What changed?"

"It just sounds weird saying 'something.'"

"But he might think it," said Ford. "I mean, this whole three-day trip thing is pretty weird."

"I know. I'm sorry."

"We're definitely getting an extra $10,000 for this."

Tilda stayed silent for a while, then said, "What about me and the car?"

Neuland said, "We already have you and the car. Right?"

Tilda looked at him and bit her lower lip for a second. She smiled. "Yeah. I guess you do."

It was a pleasant drive north, leaving the city behind and going into greenery again. Tilda played with the radio. When she first turned it on, it blared out classical music.

"It's all he ever listens to," she said. She played with the dial until she found a country station. "Is this all right?"

"It's fine by me," said Ford.

"Me too," Neuland said.

Around noon, Ford said, "Is anyone else hungry?"

"I didn't have breakfast," said Tilda. "I'm famished."

"Then pull into wherever looks good to you and we'll eat the cupboard bare."

They stopped at a little diner called The Which Way near Williams. The parking lot was crowded with cars and trucks, some from the freeway and some from the small farms that lay well off the main road. Tilda parked at the far edge of the lot, where there were several open spaces and she didn't have to worry about the Rolls getting scratched. Neuland stretched when they got out of the car and Ford sang one of the country songs they'd heard on the freeway. They headed for the diner together, Tilda walking between them.

The trio were halfway across the lot when a bearded man in a jeans jacket stepped out from behind a van and levelled a pistol at them. Neuland shoved Tilda away. She lost her balance and grabbed Ford, pulling him away from the shooter. Before Neuland could get his pistol out, the bearded man shot him three times—twice in the stomach and once in the chest. Neuland fell back against a pickup truck. The bearded man's gun had a silencer on it, so the shots were barely noticeable over the noise of the freeway. Ford left Tilda lying on the ground and rushed the shooter. The man turned, but Ford was fast. He pulled a knife from under his jacket and shoved it deep into his abdomen. The man gasped and Ford grabbed his gun hand, pointing the pistol at the ground. By now, Neuland had come around and rushed the man too. He held him from the front while Ford got behind him and, with a well-practiced motion, plunged the knife upward into the shooter's back just below the left shoulder blade, shoving it into the man's heart.

Because the gun was silenced and the view of their area of the parking lot was blocked by trucks, no one in the cafe saw the incident. Ford dragged the dead man behind the van and, with Tilda, helped Neuland back to the Rolls.

Once they'd put him in the back seat, Ford said, "Get us out of here."

Tilda looked at Neuland trying to sit up in the back. "I'll call 911," she shouted.

Ford put a hand on her shoulder and calmly said, "Calling 911 will bring cops. We don't like cops. He'll be all right. Just get us back on the road."

Tilda started the car and it squealed out of the parking lot as she aimed it at the freeway.

"Slow down," said Neuland from the back. "It's over now and everyone is all right."

"All right?" said Tilda. "You're shot."

"It's not the first time," said Ford. "The big dope."

She looked at Neuland in the rearview mirror. "You saved my life."

"You can't come to New York if you're dead," he said.

Ford said, "We need to get to a motel or something. Do you know anything around here?"

Tilda nodded, but didn't speak. There were tears in her eyes.

"You're going to be okay," said Neuland. "We're all going to be okay."

Tilda pulled into a Holiday Inn Express and got rooms for them in the back, away from the road. Then she and Ford helped Neuland upstairs and onto a king size bed in their suite. Ford brought a duffel bag with him and set it down next to Neuland.

"How are you doing?" he said.

"Better. I barely felt that shitty little 9mm he had."

"I could tell."

Ford took the bottle of goofer juice from Neuland's jacket pocket and helped him take a long gulp of the stuff.

Tilda stood at the foot of the bed with her hands balled into fists and pressed over her mouth. Neuland sat up and held a hand out to her. She reached out stiffly and took it.

"I'm all right," he said. "I just need to get these bullets out of me."

"How can you be all right?" said Tilda. She put a hand on his chest. "That one looks like it must have hit your heart."

Ford took a medical kit from the duffel bag and set it on the bed. To Neuland he said, "Do you want to do it or should I?"

"I'm all right to do it. Thanks," said Neuland as he took a set of forceps out of the kit.

Ford took hold of Tilda's arm and said, "You should go to your room. I'll come and get you when this is all over."

She looked from him to Neuland, who sat against the headboard, the forceps in his hand. He looked miserable to her.

"No. He saved my life. I want to stay and help."

"There's nothing to help with," said Neuland.

"I'd still like to stay. Please."

"Okay. But if you start to feel sick, there's no shame in puking in the bathroom."

She didn't say anything and her hands were pressed to her mouth again. Neuland took off his shirt. Then he spread the forceps apart a few centimeters and slid them into a bullet hole in his stomach. He made faces while he probed for the slug, but didn't utter a sound. After a minute or so he removed the forceps with the first bullet gripped between its teeth. There was something ochre on it that wasn't blood. Ford held out a paper coffee cup he got from on top of the mini-bar, and Neuland dropped in the bullet. Then he probed for the second shot. That one he found a lot faster, and he dropped it into the cup with the first. But the bullet in his chest was harder to reach.

After a few minutes he gave up and said, "It bounced off a rib, I think. I don't know where the hell it is."

"That's okay," said Ford. "When the job is wrapped up, we'll get you to a doctor and get some X-rays."

Neuland nodded and drained the bottle of goofer juice.

Tilda held a roll of gauze that she'd taken from the medical kit. She stared at Neuland. "You're not bleeding. I don't think that's normal."

"It is for me," he said.

"I don't understand."

Ford took the gauze from her and put it back in the kit. "That's one of the reasons we wanted you to go to your room. You don't need to see this or know about these things."

"Know about what? What's happening?"

Very gently, Neuland said, "Tilda, I'm dead. I don't bleed because my heart doesn't beat. Bullets can't kill me because I'm already there."

Tilda turned to Ford. "He's delirious," she said. "I'm calling a doctor." She pulled a phone from her shoulder bag, but Ford pushed it back in.

"Everything my partner just said is true. He's a dead man."

Tilda took a step back. "Does that mean you're dead too?"

"No. I'm alive, just like you. But understand, Neuland being dead is one of the reasons we're such a good team. We can each do things the other can't."

Tilda sagged and sat in a chair. "I don't know if you're fucking with me because you think I'm a bumpkin or what."

"Listen to me," said Neuland. "I'm what you call a *Marcheur*. I died and was brought back to life by people who do that kind of thing for a living. There are a few people like me out there, walking and working among the living. We're not much different from you. We just want to have a life like anyone else."

Tilda shook her head. "I don't know. I have to think."

"Take whatever time you need."

Ford took peroxide from the medical kit and used a hand towel from the bathroom to wipe away the reddish-black fluid from around Neuland's wounds.

"Thanks," said the dead man. Ford nodded and threw the towel into a waste basket.

"What do you think that was about back there?" he said.

"It had to be one of Garrick's people, right?" said Neuland. "There's no one in San Francisco dumb enough to try something that low class on us."

"He must have followed us from the city."

"He must have. Except I didn't see anyone."

"Me neither," said Ford. "We're going to have to be more careful until we can get out of the Bay Area."

Still in the chair, Tilda had a hand over her eyes.

"You okay?" said Ford.

When she took her hand away, her eyes were red. "I don't know," she said. "First, I'm almost shot. Then my life is saved—by a dead man—and I don't know what to do with any of that."

"I understand," said Neuland. "We're not exactly regular people."

Ford said, "Listen, if you don't want to drive us the rest of the way to Mansfield's place, it's okay. Just give us the address and we'll get there ourselves. We'll even come up with a story that will clear you and make us the assholes. Okay?"

Tilda propped her chin on her hand. "I don't know. I have to think." She got up abruptly and said, "I'm going to go now."

Ford walked her to the door and said, "If you're scared tomorrow, just slip Mansfield's address under the door and you'll never see us again."

She went outside and gave him an abrupt nod before walking down the hall.

Ford went back and sat at the end of the bed. Neuland was still propped against the headboard. He said, "Good thing she kissed us yesterday."

Neuland nodded. "No more kisses from her."

7

Later, Neuland dreamed of the swamp again. It was in the Deep South sometime in the nineteen-thirties. He'd died only recently and had woken up to the wet heat and the constant smell of rot. Rotten vegetation. Rotting animal carcasses. The rotting bodies of the city men who'd come looking for secrets and only found a quick death. Some of the bodies were resurrected while the rest were fed to the things of the swamp. Most were the ordinary wildlife Neuland had seen in books and newsreels, but others were from somewhere else entirely. Hideous things with too many eyes or arms that gnarled into toothed tentacles. Some had the heads of nightmare animals while others—the worst ones—caterwauled and screamed through clusters of tiny heads that looked like leprous children. Neuland's captors would never say exactly where the creatures came from. Some had been summoned and refused to go back where they belonged. Others simply appeared on their own, either from the bowels of the swamp itself or some other realm that the locals refused to talk about.

Because he was a big man, Neuland mostly did manual labor, moving bales of hay or crates around the hidden compound.

But because of his size and strength, he occasionally had to help drive off the nightmare things when they attacked. Those were the worst times. The times he'd wished he'd never been given a second life. However, he proved an adept hunter and killer, and that earned him both praise and extra rations of goofer juice. These made him stronger and faster, but he didn't let anyone know. Those abilities would come in handy one day and, being a patient man, Neuland was willing to wait until the right time to use them.

8

Tilda knocked on their door at precisely nine the next morning and Ford let her in. She wasn't dressed in a business suit, but casually in black slacks and a red-and-white-striped blouse, no longer pretending to be something she wasn't. When Neuland came out of the bathroom she said, "How are you today?"

"Right as rain. I just needed some rest."

"Can I ask you a question?"

"Of course."

"Did it hurt when that man shot you?"

"It did. A lot."

"But not now."

"The stuff I drink? It fixes me up quickly."

Tilda shook her head. "Most days, I think I could use some of that."

"Me too," said Ford. "Listen, we've been talking. We don't like this slow-boat-north trip, especially after what happened yesterday. We want to see Mansfield today."

Tilda frowned and looked around the room. "He won't like it. He wanted us to take another day and meet him in the morning."

"If he's mad, we'll deal with it," Ford said.

She looked at the men. "I'm sorry about running out last night."

Neuland shook his head. "That's okay. The offers still stands. If you want, we can drive ourselves."

"No. It's my job and I'm much better today." Tilda smiled pleasantly, but there was a tightness around her mouth. The men understood that after the previous night, she was likely to be a lot more reserved for the rest of the trip.

Ford and Neuland put on thin white necklaces on before they buttoned their shirts. Ford gave one to Tilda. "Put it on under your shirt, so no one can see it."

After a moment, Tilda opened the top two buttons of her blouse, but she didn't put the necklace on right away. "What's this for?"

Neuland said, "It will make it harder to track us."

Tilda examined the many segments of necklace. She said, "Are these bones?"

"Yes. Bird bones. Lizard. Amber beads with insects inside. Some other things, all strung on red thread."

"Is it magic or something?"

"Exactly."

"Like you're magic?"

Neuland thought about it. "I'm not sure I'm magic."

"What would you call a walking, talking dead man?"

"Neuland."

Tilda frowned and put on her necklace, buttoning her blouse again. "I'm sorry," she said.

"It's okay. You had the whole thing sprung on you pretty quickly."

"Points to you for not screaming and running away," said Ford. "We've seen dangerous men do it when they figured out my partner."

Neuland laughed. "Remember Robbie Erickson?"

Ford looked at Tilda. "He ran away screaming like someone put a badger down his pants."

Tilda gave them a minute smile. "You know, I've seen magic before. Not like people coming back from the dead, but magic."

"Yeah? What kind?"

"Scared kind."

Neuland said, "Like the magic scared you or the magic was for scared people."

"The second thing."

"Papa Shep, maybe?"

"Dad and grandpa too."

"Not your mother or grandmother?" said Ford.

"Grandma was a widower ever since I can remember. I don't know what happened to mom. When I brought her up Dad would get upset and Papa Shep would throw things."

"Since we'll already be there, want us to look into your mom's situation?"

Neuland came over, tying his tie. "If Papa Shep throws things at us, we'll throw them right back."

This time Tilda smiled for real. "Thank you, but I decided a while ago that it was time to let go."

Ford said, "Okay. But let us know if you change your mind. We have more than guns in these bags."

"More magic?"

"Lots."

Tilda nodded to the door. "We should probably get going."

They went downstairs together and Neuland had Tilda wait in the hotel lobby while he and Ford checked out the parking lot. When they were sure it was safe, Ford retrieved her and they drove off in the Rolls.

After a half hour on the road with country music playing on the radio, Ford said,

"Can I ask you a question?"

He was in the front seat and Tilda glanced over at him. "Sure."

"Why haven't you left home? You want to. You're smart. You didn't run off last night, so you can roll with the punches. What's keeping you there?"

"Mr. Mansfield is the head of the family. I can't just abandon my family."

"What other family do you have?" said Neuland.

"Just Mr. Mansfield."

"He controls the money, doesn't he?"

"You can say that again. There isn't a penny he doesn't know about."

"He'd cut you off if you left."

She nodded. "He takes disloyalty very seriously."

"But it's more than that, isn't it?"

"I don't know what you mean."

Ford said, "You're scared of him."

Tilda didn't reply.

"You don't have to talk about it if you don't want to."

Neuland said, "We're just trying to get a sense of the man before we meet him."

"Right," said Tilda tightly. "That's all you care about."

"No," said Ford. "Just understand that you don't have to be scared while we're around."

"I'm scared all the time. Aren't you?"

"Us? We're too dumb to be scared."

Neuland said, "I can't tie my shoes without his help."

"And I can't work a toothpaste tube."

Tilda laughed a little. "You two. Sometimes I don't know how much of what you say to believe."

"Believe this," said Neuland. "We have your back."

"I'll try."

"That's a good start," said Ford.

The men watched the road behind them to see if they were being followed but didn't see anything of note.

When they reached Red Bluff, Tilda said, "Do you mind if we stop here for a while?"

"You want to get lunch?" said Ford.

"We can do that. But I just don't want..."

"You don't want to get home too early."

"Yes."

"Would it help if you called and told him we were coming?" said Neuland.

"Mr. Mansfield doesn't like phones."

"He doesn't have one?"

"He has a phone, but I'm the only one who uses it."

Ford said, "What if we called him instead of you?"

"I'm the only one who uses the phone."

"There isn't anyone to take a message?"

"Just me."

Ford frowned and Neuland said, "Why is he scared of the phone?"

Tilda shook her head. "Mr. Mansfield is scared of his shadow." She clapped her hand over her mouth. "I shouldn't have said that."

Ford pointed to a Denny's a short distance away. "Let's stop here and have a leisurely lunch. We don't have to get to him right this minute."

"As long as we're there while it's still light," said Neuland.

Tilda said, "Why light?"

"I like to see a place before I go inside."

"It makes it easier to find the way out," said Ford.

"You think of everything," said Tilda.

"If we thought of everything, I wouldn't have gotten shot," said Neuland.

Tilda squeezed the steering wheel harder. "Do you think we're safe now?"

"I've been watching. No one is following us."

"And we have our necklaces," said Ford.

"If you're sure."

"We are."

Ford and Tilda ate lunch, had dessert, and drank pots of coffee while Neuland sipped from his bottle. They stayed until it was late afternoon. Tilda, who'd relaxed during lunch, tensed up again when it came to leave. Neuland left their waitress a hundred-dollar tip.

9

In its misery it lay on its back, its great gelatinous belly and many small, hooked legs pointed at the ceiling. Above it hung a crystal chandelier of considerable value and beauty. In the dim light that crept through holes in the thick curtains, it stared at long strands of cobwebs that hung from the crystals. When it kicked its little legs, it could make the cobwebs move to and fro in the feeble breeze. This was the kind of amusement it had been reduced to. Once a fearsome creature that made strong men piss themselves, it now thought of itself as little more than the insects it consumed, and less beautiful than the cobwebs hanging overhead. It soon rolled back onto its belly, blowing a cloud of dust from the floor. Twenty years' worth of the stuff, so that it looked like the room was caught in a light snowfall. There was something by one of its front feet. A small, colorful sphere. It kicked the thing and it bounced under a large piece of furniture used by the soft things for making pleasant tinkling sounds.

It remembered when the floor had been clean and people had filled the house. There was a festive gathering many years earlier. There were lights everywhere, strung throughout the downstairs rooms. A massive tree in the living room decorated with more lights and brightly wrapped boxes beneath. A fire blazed in the fireplace all day and night. It never lacked for food in those days. Of course, it was younger then, and more timid, so it remained invisible most of the time.

It was one night during the festivities, when the creature had been examining the tree, that it learned being visible could be quite fun. A man came down the stairs in the middle of the night and saw it, a string of fairy lights dangling from one of its small, hooked legs. The sound the man made—a scream, it learned later—was delightful. However, the incident was also so startling that it didn't eat the man at all, but merely turned invisible and returned to the basement, where it spent almost all of its time.

After that, it became visible more often, showing itself just before it ate one of the soft things, savoring the sounds they made. By then, it knew that the owners of the house were well aware of its presence. They laid traps for it with animals and food, but it wasn't foolish enough to be taken that easily. One evening it emerged from the basement and found a soft thing bound and gagged at the bottom of the stairs. It knew that what lay before it was a sacrifice, laid out to lure it into a trap. But the soft thing smelled of soap and perfume and was so tempting. It recalled that the sacrifice was one of the smaller ones. The other soft things made a funny sound when they wanted its attention. They said, "May."

Understanding that the May thing was a trap, it didn't appear to her until the last minute. The soft thing tried to scream through its gag and the creature grabbed her in its protruding mouth. That was when the other soft things sprang their trap. Tall things seemed to appear from the shadows. They carried tubes that made exploding sounds and heavy, burning balls of metal tore into its body, making it howl in agony. Again and again came the explosions, so many that it quickly retreated back to the basement.

But it took its prize—May—with it. It ate the thing quickly, in enough pain that even the soft thing's shrieks gave it no pleasure. Soon after that, the soft things abandoned the house for good.

A crashing sound from the back of the house shook the creature from its reverie. Glass breaking. Footsteps. They creeped around the kitchen, then up the back staircase to the second floor. It grew anxious at the sounds and paced through the living room and parlor, waiting for the noise to settle down. It walked over the white carpets, the white walls, and the white furniture. It sat at the bottom of the white-carpeted staircase until it heard a familiar sound from long ago—a bed spring squeaking. It squeaked for a few minutes and then stopped. The creature listened until it heard the sound of heavy, steady breathing. Then it pulled itself up the stairs, its stomach rumbling.

It stopped in the doorway of the white master bedroom where one of the soft things was asleep on the enormous, canopied bed. The creature didn't approach immediately. The soft thing smelled strange. A combination of dirt, sweat, feces, and something else—its own death. The soft thing wasn't well. There was glass embedded in the soles of its ragged shoes, remnants of the window it had broken to enter the house. This annoyed the creature. The house belonged to it, and it didn't like the idea of just anyone sneaking inside.

It ate the soft thing quickly and without pleasure. First, it stripped off its skin and swallowed it in one slippery piece. Then it sucked out the soft thing's bones and crunched them down. Finally, it feasted on the squishy internal parts that were its favorite. But the thing didn't taste quite right and even its screams couldn't improve the creature's mood.

Afterward, it sat in the bloody bedroom, not listening so much as feeling the air. Something had been coming. Something *was* coming. And it wasn't the soft thing it had just eaten. What it had felt was larger, stronger, and more dangerous. But whatever it had been, it was gone now. Then it wondered if maybe it hadn't ever been there at all. It contemplated the possibility that in its loneliness it had gone mad. It went back down the white stairs to the white living room and pushed a white curtain aside with one of its legs. Was there something out there? It hoped so, for if it knew nothing else, it knew that it was better to be hungry than to be insane.

10

Tilda turned the Rolls off the freeway and onto a two-lane side road that went into the woods. After perhaps thirty minutes, she turned them onto a paved one-lane road. It was in good condition, but weeds and other plants had grown up tall around the edges. It gave the road the feel of something long abandoned.

Another ten minutes on, the unruly landscape fell away and they found themselves in country that looked like the grounds of a wealthy landowner. There was an apple orchard and a large lake off to the left. But beyond that area, the land took on an odd look again.

They went through a thickly wooded area where the trees were decorated with voudon symbols. Beyond that dolls were nailed to tree branches, along with children's shoes. There were god's eyes, feng shui mirrors, and old traditional wards like the ones Ford had seen on a trip to England just before he started working with Neuland. There were crosses everywhere, large and small. Wooden, metal, and woven from what looked like corn husks.

Beyond the trees, the fields on both sides of the road were filled with hundreds of scarecrows, like a ragged, sun-bleached army. They passed through another thicket where another brigade of scarecrows hung from the trees. That's what it looked like, at first.

After a moment, Ford said, "Do you see this?"

"I do. Those aren't dummies."

Neuland, who was up front with Tilda said, "Why does Mansfield have a forest of corpses on his land?"

She replied, "He says it's to fool what's after him."

"Where did he get the bodies?"

"He bought them. From rural cemeteries all over the state. Plus, there are some others."

"What does that mean?" said Ford, leaning forward between them.

Tilda pointed to an enormous oak and said, "My dad and grandpa. They both committed suicide."

"Because of whoever we're looking for?"

"I'm not sure."

"I'm sorry," said Neuland.

Tilda shook her head and looked straight ahead. "I still don't understand it. I remember Dad being happy when I was a kid. Of course, things changed after Mom left."

"I'm sorry too," said Ford. "Bad things happen. Sometimes even good people give up hope."

Tilda glanced at Neuland. "I wish my dad was like you. Dead, but still alive."

"So do I," he said.

"We'll be at the house soon."

Then the road opened up. The trees fell away behind them and they finally saw the Mansfield mansion.

"What the hell is that?" said Ford.

The building was three stories tall and sprawled in all directions as if it had been dropped there from the sky. The men had expected something dark and Gothic, but what they found wasn't that at all. It was a fifties idea of modern architecture, all poured gray concrete—hundreds of tons of it—and harsh angles.

"That's not a mansion. It's a goddamn fort," said Neuland.

"It was all the rage back when it was first built. A glimpse of the neat, clean future."

Ford said, "It looks like where they fire from nukes from."

"Please don't talk like that to Mr. Mansfield," said Tilda. "He's very proud of the place."

"We'll be on our best behavior," Neuland said.

There were more charms and protections all over the enormous structure. The windows were all stained glass and they contained wards too. The only thing the men liked about the place was the row of expensive cars out front. Another Rolls-Royce. A Bugatti. A fifties T-Bird. A red sixties Cadillac convertible as big as a battleship. All the cars were covered in dust, indicating they hadn't been driven in a long time.

Tilda parked the Silver Cloud at the far end of the row and led them into the house. Ford and Neuland were relieved that the inside was a lot homier than the outside. Tilda took them into an elegant Victorian parlor full of antique furniture and family portraits on the walls. Both men stood where they were, taking in the interior that clashed so violently with the house's exterior.

"It's not a fort," whispered Ford. "It's a museum."

Neuland shook his head. "No, it is a fort." He looked at Tilda. "The concrete walls outside were built around an older house, weren't they?"

Tilda nodded and said, "You're right. It was Mr. Mansfield's idea."

"The question is, are the new walls to keep something in or something out?" said Ford.

Tilda looked uncomfortable for a moment before saying, "You'll have to ask Mr. Mansfield that."

"So, when do we meet the great man?"

"Please. You said you'd be good," said Tilda, sounding nervous.

"Not another word," said Ford.

A moment later, an old man rolled into the parlor in a motorized wheelchair. His white hair lay thin and straw-like on the gray, unhealthy skin of his scalp. The sagging skin of his face and hands was the color of pale clay. He was dressed in a silk smoking jacket with a couple of shirts beneath it, like he was cold even in the pleasantly temperate room.

Mansfield said, "I thought I heard voices. Hello, Tilda. What the hell are you doing here? I said I didn't want to see your face for two more days."

Tilda bit her lip and said, "I know, Mr. Mansfield, but you see..."

Neuland said, "It's not her fault. We insisted."

"We were tired of sitting on our asses."

Mansfield stared at the men. "So, this is them?"

"Yes, sir."

He looked down his nose. "Are you sure? They don't look like killers. They look like a couple of cheap pimps."

Ford and Neuland laughed.

"Please," said Tilda. "You see, something happened on the way up from the city."

Ford said, "There was an incident. We had to kill a man who'd followed us."

"Poor Tilda was there to see it," said Neuland. "But you should be proud of her. She was over it fast and got us to a hotel where we could order room service and watch cartoons."

Mansfield gave them a sour smile. "What an exciting tale.

But I'm paying you good money to do what I say, and I said not to come until tomorrow."

"Tilda said you were worried about your someone knowing we're here. You don't have to be. We're not new to this game. We know how to cloak ourselves."

"Yes? Show me."

Neuland, Ford, and Tilda unbuttoned their shirts and showed Mansfield their bone necklaces.

He waved a dismissive hand. "Voodoo rubbish."

"We're here now," said Ford. "Do you want us or not? If not, we'll take our money and go."

Mansfield pointed a bony finger at them. "Which one of you is the dead man?"

"That would be me," said Neuland.

Looking him up and down, Mansfield said, "A real-life dirt-napper in my home. Goodness gracious. You disgust me, you know. But right now, I'd give anything to be one of you."

Neuland said, "If you don't mind me asking, how do you even know about people like me? We don't exactly advertise."

Mansfield made a scoffing sound. "Is your brain rotten too? Look around the house, you idiot. You think I dabble in magic like some Las Vegas pud-puller? I know what I know because I need to know it."

"And you have money to buy the information," said Ford.

"Money is a tool," said Mansfield. "It's a weapon, too. Don't ever forget that."

"That's not a very friendly thing to say," said Neuland.

"No," said Ford. "Insults we'll take, but not threats. Go be an asshole on your own time."

The men turned and headed back to the front door.

"Come back here, you bastards," shouted Mansfield.

"Fuck you," replied Ford.

"Talk to them, Tilda," said Mansfield.

Neuland turned but kept walking. "Leave her out of this. Oh, and we're taking one of your cars. We'll leave it at the airport."

"Goddamn you all."

"Please, Mr. Mansfield…" said Tilda.

"Goddamn every one of you."

"Sweet talker," said Ford.

Just as the men reached the door, Mansfield shouted, "A hundred thousand."

Ford opened the front door.

"Two hundred thousand."

Ford turned and said, "Each."

Mansfield shook his head. "You're worse than the Jew."

"What are you talking about?" said Neuland.

Pointing at Tilda, Mansfield said, "The one who married this one's mother."

"Do we have a deal?" said Ford.

"Of course. But you don't ever get to tell me how to talk again."

"Fair enough."

The old man turned to Tilda. "I'm taking these pricks to the chapel. You stay here and put on coffee or something. Make yourself useful for once."

Ford took a deep breath and Neuland balled his fists. Neither one cared for how Mansfield treated Tilda. It made them happy to soak the old man for every cent they could.

Mansfield took a large silver crucifix from his pocket and put it around his neck. Then he led them out the back of the house and down a wheelchair ramp. Beyond that was a smooth concrete walkway from the back porch to a small chapel in a nearby grove of trees.

"You always wear that cross when you leave the house?" said Ford.

"It's more useful than the filthy voodoo nonsense around your necks."

"How do you know?" Neuland said.

"Because this belonged to Clement VI. Ever heard of him?"

"The plague pope. He hid behind a wall of burning logs hoping it would keep the plague from taking him."

"And it worked."

"The flames kept the fleas away. It wasn't magic."

"So you say. Besides, even if it wasn't magic, he was the luckiest fucker ever to wear one of those ridiculous papal hats. Half of Europe died around him horribly, but he slipped away in his nice, soft bed at sixty-one. A pretty good run for someone back then, wouldn't you say?"

"You like him because he's like you," said Ford. "Hunkered down in his palace waiting for the boogieman to go away."

"It worked. He had a good long life."

Ford shrugged. "If that's what you call a life."

Mansfield shot him a look, but didn't say anything. "It's just up ahead."

The chapel he led them to was nothing to look at. A simple white wooden building with a weathered wooden cross on top. All the shutters were closed, so the men couldn't see inside. There was a wildly out of place keypad on the wall next to the chapel's old doors. Mansfield made the men look away while he punched in the code to unlock the building. Then the old man rolled back so that Ford and Neuland had to open the doors and go inside first.

It was dark in the chapel, and they still couldn't see very much. Mansfield rolled in behind them and said, "Close the damn doors." Neuland did, and the moment they were shut, automatic lights came on.

Even the rows of scarecrows and hanged men in the trees didn't prepare Ford and Neuland for what they saw. The walls of the chapel were painted rusty red with something that didn't look like paint. Dried animal carcasses hung from the ceiling, along with crosses and hundreds of little air fresheners in the shape of pine trees. The altar at the far end of the chapel was made of bones. Wards, charms, crosses, and Milagros painted and nailed up all around it. Flayed human skins were stretched over the shuttered windows.

"I see you admiring my curtains," said Mansfield, laughing to himself. "Don't worry. We didn't kill any of them. They're wretches from a sanitarium down the road. It closed many years ago. The sanitarium's owners let us borrow some of the patients as workers around the estate. For their rehabilitation, you understand. Some weren't in the best of health and died on the property. The sanitarium never asked about them, so my father would bring them into the chapel, where they could finally make something of their wasted lives."

The men didn't say said anything. They looked over the obscure symbols stained into the carpeted floor where there would normally be pews. More symbols and sigils, near the altar, were set into the bare wood floor in silver.

"What do you think, gentlemen?"

"It's a goddamn freak show," said Ford. "You could sell tickets."

Neuland said, "Kids would love this at Halloween."

"I thought men such as yourselves would appreciate the kind of deep magic expressed here, but since you don't, you'll kindly keep your mouths shut about it. This is family business."

Neuland said, "Is this how you made your fortune? With a little help from the Otherworld?"

"You don't need to know that."

"Does Tilda know what's in here?"

Mansfield gave a rasping laugh. "That dull child still believes in Santa and the cookie monster."

Ford said, "It's not *the* cookie monster. It's just Cookie Monster. That's its name."

"Do you think I give one single fuck?"

"What about all those bodies in the trees?" said Neuland. "What did you tell Tilda about those?"

"Only what she needed to know."

"She said her father is out there," said Ford, picking up what looked like a glove, but was the skin from a human hand. He dropped it back on the altar. "You left her father out there hanging from a tree like buzzard food. That's a bit cold."

"It's what the fool deserved," Mansfield muttered.

"What happened to her mother?" said Neuland.

The old man shook his head. "May? She ran off. She was always flighty. Her husband, the Jew, was a weak man. He hanged himself a week or so after she left. That's why he's, as you said, buzzard food."

"Tilda was unclear about something when she hired us," said Ford. "She said both *someone* or *something* was after you. Which is it?"

"Something, of course. It's what drove us out of Pale House."

"What's Pale House?" said Neuland.

"Our first family home in this country. A century and a half old. The damned devil drove us out."

Ford started to laugh, but Neuland put a hand on his arm. He said, "When you say devil, do you mean *the* devil?"

"Of course I mean *the* devil. Who else?" said Mansfield angrily.

Neuland opened and closed his hands. He said, "Where I'm from, I've been around people who saw devils every day. But that's just what they called the creatures they dealt with and what the creatures sometimes called themselves. I've met dozens of devils in my time. But never *the* devil. If he exists, I think he has bigger fish to fry than your clan."

Mansfield gave him another sour smile, "I guess a dead man would know all about those things. Tell me, did you meet god while you were sucking dirt?"

"If he stopped by, I missed him."

"Pity. He might have taught you some manners."

"They wouldn't have stuck."

"How exactly did the devil drive you out?" said Ford.

"He's a hungry bastard. He eats everything. Anything."

"Why is he after you?"

"It's a family curse. An old one."

Ford looked around the chapel. "I take it you tried getting rid of him yourself?"

"How clever you are," said Mansfield. "Why didn't we think of that? Of course we tried, you prick. We used what conjurations and exorcisms we knew, and when that didn't work, we brought in every sort of witch, psychic, local injuns with smudge sticks, a Satanist priest, even a troop of goddamn gypsies. A circus of useless shit stains, every one of them. None could budge the beast."

"It always outwitted you."

"We almost got it once. Laid a trap for it. Trussed up and left out a tasty morsel for it. I hired every cowboy and sharpshooter in the area. They blasted that thing with bullets of silver and lead and gold. One lunatic even had a shotgun that worked like a flame thrower."

"A Dragon's Breath load," said Neuland.

"It wasn't much of a dragon," said Mansfield. "The devil ate our morsel and injured some of the men before we got out."

"What was the morsel you used to attract it?"

"Why?" said Mansfield suspiciously.

"Maybe we'll want to use the same trick."

The old man looked into the distance. "It was a long time ago. I don't remember."

"Was it alive?"

"Definitely. The devil doesn't care for dead things," he said and looked at Neuland. "I guess you're safe, dodo."

"Lucky me," he said. Neuland went on, "Tell me this, Mr. Mansfield. This situation has been going on for years, right?"

"Yes."

"Why do you want the devil driven out of Pale House now?"

Mansfield sagged in his chair a little. "I'm old and I'm sick. I grew up in that house. It's where I want to die."

"Did it ever occur to you that the devil is why May ran away?"

"You're not here for her. She's long gone."

Ford picked up the flayed hand again and tossed it at Mansfield's feet. "How long has your family had such baroque hobbies?"

"You don't need to know that. And keep your opinions about my family to yourself if you want to see your money."

"Sure thing," said Ford, but left the hand where it lay.

Mansfield said, "I'm tired. All this talk wears me out. I'm going to my room. Since you pricks are here early, I suppose you'll be spending the night."

"Or you could give us our money and we'll give you your privacy."

"Fat chance. Come inside. Tilda will take you to the guest rooms."

~

Later that night, when the men were alone in Ford's room, he said, "How much of what the old man said do you believe?"

Neuland said, "I believe there's something dangerous in Pale House. But not much beyond that."

"What about the family curse nonsense?"

"Not a word of that. Whatever the devil is, Mansfield or someone else in the family called it up."

Ford said, "Yeah, but how? Do you think these clowns are capable of calling up a real demon?"

"Probably not on purpose. It might be as simple as a fuckup at a ritual."

"Idiots playing with what they don't understand."

"Or maybe they raised it, then tried to get rid of it, and it decided it didn't want to go."

"If that's true, Mansfield will never admit it."

"That's what bothers me," said Neuland. "Not that he might have lied to us, but knowing he's holding something back."

Ford frowned. "There's a lot of that going around these days."

"Tell me about it. After this, no more weirdo jobs. Just clients who point out the target and say, 'Sic 'em.'"

"A little simplicity would be nice."

Neuland said, "I don't trust anything about this place or that old man. I'll keep an eye on things while you sleep."

"Like hell you will. We do this by the book. I'll do two hours and come and knock on your door. Anything tries to get in but me, kill it."

"Amen to that."

11

In the morning, the men emptied their duffels bags on Neuland's bed and began sorting through their weapons and equipment.

"Knock knock," Tilda said, standing in the doorway. "May I come in?"

"Of course," said Ford. "We're just gearing up."

"So I see." She watched them load their guns for a moment. Each man carried two pistols in shoulder holsters. Neuland had a semi-automatic rifle and Ford had a shotgun. Tilda said, "Are guns all you're taking? Mr. Mansfield told me that bullets didn't work on the devil."

Smiling, Ford said, "They didn't have our kind of bullets."

"These are customs loads," said Neuland. "Some purchased and some homemade."

"What does 'custom load' mean?"

"All these bullets are special. Handmade. Some made from cold iron. Some from the bark of a white ash tree, or carved from the bones of a saint. Others dipped in a variety of potions."

Ford ratcheted his shotgun. "I have shells with holy water. Some with phosphorous to burn it. A couple of UV shots."

"What are those?" said Tilda.

Neuland said, "They hit you and explode into light. It sounds like people have only seen your devil inside. Maybe it doesn't like anywhere bright."

She pointed to some goggles on the bed. "I'm guessing those aren't ordinary either."

"Right. They'll show us the auras of anything in the house. Once we detect what it is, we'll have a better idea of how to take it down. Remember, I kill the living."

"And I kill the dead. Whatever that thing is, we'll stop it fast," said Ford.

Tilda picked up the goggles. "Can I try them?"

"Be my guest."

She put them on over her head and looked at Ford. He was ringed by bright yellow light. When Tilda looked at her hands, they glowed the same way. Neuland, however, was a grayish purple, and it was a disturbing reminder of exactly what he was. She took the goggles off and placed them carefully back onto the bed. She said, "So, what's your plan?"

"We go to Pale House, find your devil, and kill it."

"That's it?"

"It's all we can do at the moment," said Neuland. "We don't know enough about it to be clever. So, we go in and let it know we're there. With luck, we'll draw it out into a direct attack."

"And blast it to kitty litter," said Ford.

Tilda picked up a bottle lying on a pillow. When she looked inside, dozens of small eyes stared back at her. She dropped it back where it was. "I thought you'd have a more complicated strategy," Tilda said.

"We have backup plans. We always do," said Neuland.

"Good. I mean, after all the stories, I'm worried and wouldn't want anything to happen, you know, to you."

"Thank you. But don't worry. We've done things like this a hundred times."

"Okay then. When you're ready, I'll drive you to Pale House. It's just a couple of miles up the road."

The men wore their black suit pants, but left their jackets on the backs of a couple of chairs. They checked their pistols one more time and slung their long guns over their shoulders.

Ford looked at Tilda. "If you're ready, we're ready."

She took a breath and said, "Mr. Mansfield wants to see you on the way out."

"Lucky us," said Neuland dryly.

Tilda was right. Mansfield was waiting for them in his wheelchair at the bottom of the stairs. He looked them over and said, "A couple of real GI Joes, aren't you?"

"Do you want us to salute you or something?" said Ford.

"I just want you to do your job."

"Then let us go do it."

"Where's the money Tilda already gave you?"

"Why?" said Neuland.

"If you're complete fuckups and get eaten, I want it back."

"It's in a box at the bottom of one of the duffle bags. But don't bother touching it unless you're sure we're dead."

"Why? Is it booby trapped?"

"Very much."

Mansfield frowned. "A couple of pimps to the end."

The men went out the front door and Tilda followed. They piled into the Rolls-Royce and she drove them away from Mansfield's fortress.

~

Pale House was a lot more what they'd expected when they'd first gone down the road to Mansfield's home. It was an imposing, three-story Victorian mansion with turrets and gables, a porch around the front and a rooster weathervane above the chimney. But what was most striking about it was that it was all white. Every inch of the wooden sides, up to the snow-colored shingles on the roof. Having been all but abandoned years before, a lot of the white was dingy and streaked with dirt and mildew. Still, it glowed brightly in the early morning sunlight.

"I can see how it got its name," said Neuland.

"Is the inside as white as the outside?" said Ford.

"Yep. Every inch," said Tilda. "Even the furniture."

"Whose idea was that?"

"I guess great-great-granddad, or maybe great-great-great. I don't know much about the house or the family that far back. Mr. Mansfield doesn't talk about them. Anyway, everything is white to show off to all the other landowners who used to live around here. I mean, you can imagine how hard it was to keep a house that white and gleaming all the time. There was a huge staff that cleaned and generally kept up the place."

"Conspicuous consumption," said Neuland.

"I don't like it," said Ford. "No offense, but that's one goddamn ugly house."

"What's it like inside?" said Neuland.

Tilda said, "I barely remember it. It's been locked up since I was a little girl. I mostly remember playing there with Mom and Dad. I was maybe three."

"There were no devils back then? No hint of them?"

"Not that I remember. Of course, everything happened so fast. We lived there, then suddenly, we all moved out. I guess some of the staff were the devil's early victims. After that, the rest of the workers quit and we locked the place up tight."

"And you all moved into the house up the road?"

"Yes. That was Mr. Mansfield's project. He hated Pale House. Considered it too old fashioned."

"So he built Fort Knox," said Ford.

"I suppose so. Like I said, a lot of the memories are vague, but I do remember them building the new house and being puzzled why no one would talk about why we needed it."

They stopped out front of Pale House and Tilda led them over the porch. She opened a large padlock, took a chain off the front doors, and started to reach for the doorknob. Ford caught her hand and pushed it away before opening the door himself. For a moment, the three of them waited on the porch, just listening. Soon, Neuland put on his goggles, and Ford followed suit. They entered the house with their pistols drawn. They were only a few steps inside when Neuland pointed down to where the dust had been disturbed on the floor.

"There's definitely something here," he said. "At least the old man isn't completely crazy."

"I generally prefer crazy to devils," said Ford.

"Devils we can kill. Crazy doesn't always pay up."

"Good point."

They went farther into the living room and parlor, examining the tracks.

"You ever seen anything like those prints before?" said Ford.

"Never. We're dealing with something unique."

"I hate unique."

"Me too."

The two men turned around to follow the tracks back the way they'd come and found Tilda standing in the entranceway, across from the white staircase.

"No," said Neuland.

"Hell no," said Ford. "Listen, you can't be in here. It's too dangerous."

"Even if I stay right by the door? Please. I haven't seen the house in years."

"When we're done you can have a birthday party, throw a rave, or open a hotel. But until then, you really need to leave."

But Tilda remained by the stairs, looking around. Neuland spotted something on the ground, under a white grand piano. He picked it up and brought it back to her. "Is this yours?"

It was a small rubber ball, shaped like a soccer ball, but each segment was a different color.

"Oh yes! Yes, it is. Thank you."

"Why don't you take it and go back to the other house? We'll call you when we're finished."

She held the ball in both hands. "That's okay. I'll wait outside in case you need me."

"Sure," said Ford. "I don't think this will take long. From the look of these tracks, your devil is big. We'll spot it in a second."

"That makes me feel better," said Tilda. She half-smiled. "I'll be right outside."

When she was gone, the men put their goggles back on and began searching the house.

12

S lumbering in the basement, it heard something overhead. The gentle padding of feet. Then voices. It lumbered around in the dark and walked to the staircase, listening carefully. No. It hadn't imagined it. There were soft things in the house. One, two, three of them. And so soon after the one it had eaten in the upstairs bedroom. It wondered if they knew the bedroom thing and were looking for it. Perhaps not. They seemed to have come through the front doors, not a window. No matter. The sounds of life made it hungry again, so it turned invisible and started up the stairs.

13

There were tracks everywhere, so they made a circuit of the first floor, starting in the parlor, then through the dining room to the kitchen. They checked the pantry, the back stairs, and bathroom. All they found was dust, overturned furniture, and some empty teacups and plates of desiccated food from when the family had fled the house. What was peculiar to them was that they didn't see a trace of even a single mouse or insect.

They went back to the front of the house, but before heading up the grand white staircase Neuland nodded to a brown patch on the floor. "There's something here. Blood spatter."

Ford scratched the wood at the bottom of the stairs with his fingernail. "And a lot of it," he said. "I think this is what professionals call evidence."

"Our devil is a hungry thing," replied Neuland. "No mice. No insects. It could make a living as an exterminator."

"I should have had a protein bar before we left," said Ford, frowning.

"You're hungry?" said Neuland.

"I could kill and skin a moose."

At the top of the stairs, Neuland slowly opened the first door they came across. There was nothing inside but a dusty bed and some fly-specked furniture. "Too bad that old golem was waiting for us," he said. "I'm sure they had a nice breakfast laid out somewhere in the house."

"That asshole. If you ask me, he's the devil of whatever the hell he calls that cinderblock he lives in."

"We can get Tilda to drive us to the nearest town for a celebration dinner once we're done."

Ford said, "I'm going to have a steak. I'm going to have two steaks."

He pushed open another door. It was just like the previous room. In fact, all the bedrooms were alike. Until they opened the master bedroom.

"Well, now the damn thing is just showing off," said Neuland.

The bed was nearly red with dried blood. It had soaked into the blankets and splashed up onto the walls and canopy. There was more blood down the side and on the floor, where there was a single, ragged shoe.

"This is recent," said Ford examining the blanket.

"That might be a problem. What if the thing isn't hungry anymore?"

"Something as big as this looks? I bet it's always hungry."

There were strange, bloody footprints on the floor and walls.

"I wish I knew what the hell these footprints fit," said Ford.

"It sure isn't here now," said Neuland. "It's too big to miss."

"Let's finish this floor and the next, then go back down. From the look of these prints, whatever this thing is, it's too big to be comfortable in the attic as well."

"We should have asked Tilda if there was a basement."

"Of course there's a basement. These old places always have spooky basements for all the canning and jarring and whatever the hell else rich country jerks do to amuse themselves."

"Right. These two floors, then the spooky basement."

Ford said, "If we don't find anything there, we might have to do a ritual. I forgot my chalk. Do you have yours?"

"Of course. Because you always forget yours."

"Showoff."

There was nothing in any of the other bedrooms on the second floor. They found more dried blood in the hallway and on the staircase to the third floor, but it looked very old. After a quick check of the attic, they gave up and went back downstairs.

Tilda was waiting in the doorway with the ball in her hand. "Anything?" she said.

Neuland pushed up his goggles and said, "It's definitely been here recently. That means it's almost certainly still around."

"How do you know it's been here?"

"It killed someone within the last couple of days."

"Oh god."

"Don't worry. It's no one you knew," said Ford. "From the shoe we found, it was probably a drifter who broke in looking for someplace to sleep."

"You should go back outside," said Neuland. "We're going to check the basement, and if there's nothing there, we're going to do a ritual."

"What kind?" said Tilda.

"A summoning. A small one."

Ford said, "Not enough to call up any new devils. Just expose any that are already here."

"I'd like to see that."

Neuland shook his head and Ford said, "I tell you what. When we've bagged your Pale House creep, we'll go back to Fort Knox and show you how it works where it's safe."

"But until then, you really should go back to the car," said Neuland.

"All right. But if you're not back in a half hour, I'm coming to look for you."

"Make it an hour."

"Fine."

"You don't have anything to eat in the car, do you?" said Ford.

"I'm afraid not."

"Damn. When we're done here, we're buying you a steak dinner in town."

Tilda brightened. "I'd like that."

"All right. We'll see you in two shakes of a devil's tail."

Tilda went back to the car and the men walked around the first floor until they found the basement just off the kitchen. The door was open and the dust had been disturbed.

"Bingo," said Neuland. He slid his goggles back into place, flipped on the light switch, and pointed his pistols down the stairs.

"See anything?" said Ford.

"Just more footprints."

"Then let's get this over with."

Though it was sometimes part of their job, neither man enjoyed searching rooms with only one exit. Neuland led the way downstairs while Ford went after him, watching the hall behind so nothing could sneak up on them.

When they reached the bottom of the staircase, they didn't find anything but rusting tools, canned food, and jarred preserves. There was a chute in one corner of the room with a large pile of coal at the bottom.

"Look at the floor. It's nearly clean," said Ford.

"It lives down here most of the time."

"Then where is it now?"

"To hell with all this prowling," said Neuland. "Let's do the ritual."

"Agreed."

They went back upstairs and walked the living room and parlor to determine the center point of the first floor. It was right at the bottom of the stairs. Neuland put his guns back in their holsters and began sketching out a nine-foot circle with a piece of red chalk. When the large circle was complete, he drew a second smaller circle inside it, then began filling the spaces between them with angelic and demonic names and sigils. When the summoning circle was complete, Neuland stepped out and said, "Do we want to do this the smart way or the fast way?"

"I'm hungry and I want to be done with Mansfield ASAP. Let's do it fast."

"Then you're up."

Ford holstered his guns and stepped into the circle. He took out his knife and pricked the end of his right forefinger. Blood dripped into the center of the circle which, through their goggles, turned a bright violet. Both men began a quiet chant in Latin.

Something stirred in the air.

Light flickered in the parlor. Something like static prickled the backs of their necks.

"What the hell am I seeing?" said Ford.

"I have no idea."

The front door swung open and Tilda came in. "I forgot to tell you something..." she said, and then she was screaming.

Neuland and Ford pushed back their goggles and finally saw it. Huge and gelatinous, rearing back with its legs kicking in the air, its protruding mouth lunging for Tilda. They pulled their pistols and began shooting. The creature fell back against a side table, splintering it under its weight. The men kept shooting. The creature flinched as each shot hit home, but it never stopped moving. When their pistols were empty, Ford took off his shotgun and pumped round after round into the creature. As he shot, Neuland angled around so that he was in front of Tilda, pushing her to the door with his back. Ford followed them until, just before the three of them exited Pale House, he shot the UV slug into the creature dead-center. It lit up inside and let out a hideous wail, flailing around and crushing the piano before fleeing back in the direction of the basement.

Neuland closed the doors behind them and all three jumped off the porch. Tilda was pale and the men were both cursing.

"Was that the devil?" shouted Tilda.

"It wasn't the ghost of Jack Benny," said Ford.

"I-I," stammered Tilda. "I never really believed it. I always thought it was some crazy family story. A cover-up for something else."

"It's real all right," said Neuland.

"But you didn't see it when I came in," said Tilda.

"Not until you screamed."

"What does that mean?"

"I'm not exactly sure."

"But it's dead, right? I mean, you shot it like a hundred times."

"I doubt it's dead," said Ford. "In fact, I'm pretty certain it's not."

Tilda said, "But it screamed at the end when you shot it with light."

"Yeah, the shots hurt, but it's not dead."

"How are you so sure?"

"Because it's something we haven't seen before," said Neuland. "It's not alive or dead. If it was, the goggles would have picked it up."

"If it's not alive or dead, how are you going to kill it or get rid of it or whatever?" said Tilda.

"I don't know," said Ford. "We need to think about this."

"What the hell did that old man conjure up?" said Neuland.

"Old man?" said Tilda. "Mr. Mansfield? You think he did this?"

"Don't tell him I said anything, because we're not one-hundred-percent sure."

"But it's possible," said Ford.

"It killed part of my family."

"We know. But until we understand this thing more, we need you to keep what we said secret. Can you do that?"

Tilda looked down at the driveway. "Sure. Whatever will help."

"Good. Now take us back to the house," said Neuland. "We have some thinking to do."

14

I t made a sound like the squishing, cracking noise the soft things made when it turned them inside out. This was its cry of pain and despair. It lay on its side in the dark basement, unmoving and completely visible because being invisible took too much energy. The soft things upstairs had hurt it as much as anything back home. It felt a swell of pain and loneliness.

Its home was a wet and fetid place full of creatures that, in its opinion, were far worse than it. Food had been plentiful, but much more difficult to catch and consume compared to the things in this world. The soft things weren't poisonous and they didn't spit acid into its eyes when it swallowed them.

When it first found itself snatched by some strange force into this new world, it was afraid. It didn't know how or why it was here. But then it found the soft things. So slow and stupid. So tasty and such easy prey. Chasing and feasting on them had been a delightful game, so much so that its greatest desire was to free itself of the magic that kept it bound to the house, venture out, and devour this world entirely.

But that dream might be over now. It was all alone in the dark and the quiet with nothing but its anger and pain. In its frustration, it swayed to its feet and hurled itself headfirst into the wall, shaking the foundations of the house. It fell back and cried out.

The only thing that kept it from destroying itself was the knowledge that the soft things upstairs would return one day. Perhaps to fight it, or, after enough time had passed and they felt safe, reclaim the house, sure it was dead.

It was patient enough to wait and find out which. It hoped for another fight. It hadn't fought in so long and it ached for the feel of feeding after crushing an enemy. And when it was rid of the intruders it would find a way out of this wretched prison and swallow every living thing it came across, because even through all the loneliness and pain, it liked this world. It *desired* it. It would never leave.

15

Mansfield was in the parlor when they got back. He looked up from a book and said, "That was quick. You're not entirely useless after all."

"It's not dead," said Neuland.

"Yet," said Ford.

Mansfield slammed the book shut and tossed it on a table. "Goddamn you."

"Calm down. Your devil wasn't as simple a thing as you made it sound."

"But we know what it is now and how to deal with it," Neuland said.

"You better, or I want my money back and I'll shit on you both from here to Timbuktu. You won't get a job swatting mosquitoes."

The men headed upstairs.

Mansfield said, "Go with them, Tilda. See that they're working and not jerking off. Also, make them show you this alleged money box."

"Yes, sir."

Upstairs, Tilda went into Neuland's room, where he and Ford were sitting on a couple of antique chairs with lace doilies on their backs. When he saw Tilda, Ford said, "If you want to see the money box, it's in that bag."

"I don't care about that," she said. "I just wanted to get away from Mr. Mansfield."

"Do you think he knows what the devil is, and is holding back?" said Neuland thoughtfully.

"Yes. But why?" said Ford.

"If we knew more about the damn thing, we could probably answer that."

Tilda said, "You said you knew how to kill it now, right?"

Neuland shook his head. "I was lying."

"Whatever it is, it's new to us," said Ford.

Tilda sat on the bed with the equipment.

Neuland said, "What's not dead or alive?"

"What's in between those two things?"

Neuland thought for a minute. "Something mechanical. But, in this case, also organic."

"You think it's a machine?" said Tilda.

"No," said Ford. "Mechanical in the sense that it's something from the Otherworld with a specific, simple purpose there. Here, though, it's a nightmare."

Neuland said, "Back home, the devil could be a garbage disposal for all we know."

"Which brings us back to: why is it here?"

"And more importantly, what do we do with it?'

Tilda said, "Can't you just send it back?"

"We could try that," said Neuland. "But it seems to have some level of free will. What if it doesn't want to go back?"

"We need to figure out how to kill it, even though it can't be killed," said Ford.

The three of them sat in silence for a minute. Then Tilda said,

"Do you need to know both things right now? I mean, can't you just try one, like sending it back, and see if that works?"

Neuland said, "I was wondering the same thing."

"We need to do something. I'm pissed off," said Ford.

"Not to mention embarrassed."

"Great," said Tilda. "Then let's go back and send it to hell."

Ford held up his hands to her. "Whoa, Annie Oakley. Let's calm down a minute."

"No. You just said you don't really know what you're doing. That means you could use help."

"It isn't your job to help us," said Neuland.

"I'm not. I'm helping me." Tilda got up off the bed. "I'm sure the devil is why Mom left. And Mom leaving is why Dad killed himself. I want that thing dead as much as Mr. Mansfield. More."

Ford thought for a moment and said, "I hate to say it, but having you there might help."

Neuland sat back in his chair. "You see, we were in the house a long time and it looks like the devil just stood there, only a few feet away."

"Why didn't it attack us?"

"Why?" said Tilda.

"Maybe because it knew you were there, and it was waiting. The family called it so you might be first on the menu."

"But you said it ate a stranger upstairs."

"He was alone," said Neuland. "If you'd been with him, it might have gone for you first."

"Then I'm coming along."

"You're sure you want to be bait?"

"Whatever will help get rid of it. But there's one thing. I want a gun."

Ford squinted at her. "You only used one once and you shot at the water. You think you're ready to maybe shoot a living thing?"

"You said it wasn't alive."

"You know what I mean."

"I'm ready."

"Guns weren't much help last time," said Neuland.

Ford looked at him. "The UV shell seemed to annoy it." He looked back to Tilda. "Do you know how to use a shotgun?"

She gave him a slightly curdled grin. "I never shot a pistol 'til the other day with you, but I used to go out and shoot the heads off the scarecrows with some of the neighbor kids. Of course, we didn't know what they really were back then."

Ford smiled back at her. "A natural born killer."

"I could learn," she said, picking up the shotgun from the bed.

"Mansfield isn't going to like this," said Neuland.

Tilda ratcheted the gun once. "I don't care. I'm tired of doing everything he says."

The men joined her at the bed and Neuland handed her some shotgun shells, watching carefully as she loaded the weapon. "Perfect," he said.

"Told you."

Ford and Neuland emptied the bag they'd taken with them last time and filled it with newly loaded weapons, plus an assortment of magical instruments and potions.

Ford said to Tilda, "You ready?"

She said, "Let's go kill that thing."

On their way out of the room, Neuland took the shotgun from her and handed her the duffel bag. He said, "I'll give it back outside. No use provoking the old man now."

Mansfield was waiting for them as they came back downstairs. "Heading back for another ass-kicking?"

"You seem kind of pleased for a man who wants the devil gone so much," said Ford.

Mansfield took a breath. "I take no joy in knowing that thing is out there. But I do enjoy a couple of loudmouths getting what's coming to them."

"What's coming to us is four hundred thousand dollars."

"Then earn it. You fuck up again, the price goes back down to two hundred. After that, you get car fare back to the city and not a cent more." Mansfield looked at Tilda holding the duffel. "Since when are you their pack mule?"

"I'm just helping, Mr. Mansfield."

"You drive the car and nothing more. Let these pimps carry their own toys."

Neuland took the bag from her, and he and Ford headed for the door.

Tilda hung back and said, "You're horrible sometimes."

As she followed the men out, Mansfield shouted after her. "Wait until you're my age, shitting in a bag, and glued to a chair like this. Then you can give me your opinion. Until then, shut your damn mouth."

Tilda slammed the door and drove them back to Pale House.

16

When they arrived, Ford and Neuland made Tilda wait by the car as they set things up.

Inside Pale House, they used pink Tibetan salt to make a binding circle on the floor and placed that within a square. Then they arranged ritual objects at the four corners—rattlesnake skin, candles, bones of a black dog, and a machete. Next to the candles, they placed a piece of vellum with the names of the four doors to the Otherworld, each under a small bottle of whiskey. "I hope this thing is a drinker," said Ford when he was done. While he made small adjustments to the ritual objects, Neuland went out to Tilda.

"You're on," he said.

"What do I do?"

"It's simple. You stand in the circle. Breathe deeply. Try to clear your mind and relax."

"Sure. Simple."

"We'll handle everything else."

"Meaning what?"

"We're going to trap it in the circle and torch it with consecrated gasoline."

"Wait. What the hell?"

Ford came outside, wiping salt off his hands. He said, "You can consecrate pretty much anything if you know the right people. And have the money to pay them."

"I want the devil gone, but I don't want to burn the house down."

"The house will be fine with the creature in the circle," said Neuland. "Once it catches fire, that should open a door to the Otherworld and it'll fall right through."

"What if it doesn't?"

"We'll at least have it trapped in the circle."

"Are you sure?"

"For once, yes," said Ford. "It's a creature of the Otherworld and bound by its rules."

Neuland said, "But—if anything goes wrong, start blasting with that shotgun and get out of the house."

"We've left a small space in the squared circle for the creature to enter. The moment it does, you jump out and we'll torch it," Ford said. "We have to move fast. Once you're inside, it could attack at any second."

Neuland handed Tilda a lighter. "Are you ready for this?"

She rocked on her heels once, gripped the shotgun tighter, and said, "Let's go."

The men entered the house first and got in their places— Neuland on one side, ready to close the circle with more salt, and Ford nearby with the gasoline.

"Come in," said Ford, and Tilda entered the house, moving quickly to the center of the circle.

"What happens now?" she said.

"Light the candles."

Tilda sparked the lighter and lit three of the candles. The moment the fourth one caught, there was a roar from the basement and the sound of something pounding up the stairs.

"Get ready," said Neuland.

A moment later, the enormous creature was in the room, racing at Tilda.

"Wait for it," said Ford. "Wait."

As it sped into the salted circle on its clawed legs, Neuland shouted, "Now!"

Tilda jumped backward, lost her balance, and fell, cracking her head on the floor. But Neuland quickly closed the circle behind the creature, trapping it. Ford helped Tilda up and the three of them surveyed their handiwork. The creature roared and slammed itself against the invisible barrier that held it within the circle.

"It worked," said Tilda happily.

Ford bumped her shoulder with his. "We couldn't have done it without you." He held up the bottle of gasoline. "You want to do the honors?"

Tilda smiled and said, "My hands are still shaking. You do it."

"Sure thing." Ford yelled to the creature, "Bon voyage, you fuck."

As he opened the bottle, the house began to make a noise. The timbers creaked and, from overhead, the crystal chandelier tinkled louder and louder. From the kitchen came the sounds of glassware and cans falling off shelves. The noise increased in volume as all of Pale House began to shake.

"Earthquake," shouted Tilda. "A big one."

As Ford struggled to open the tight cap on the gasoline bottle, a timber fell from the ceiling, slamming into the floor. It drove all the way through it and into the basement, breaking one side of the salt circle. Freed, the furious creature extended its long mouth and grabbed the first thing it could get to—Ford. He screamed as the creature swallowed his right arm up to the elbow.

Tilda began shooting UV rounds into the creature's body until the shotgun was empty. Neuland grabbed one of the machetes and swung it down on the creature's wriggling mouth, severing several feet of it and freeing Ford, who collapsed on the floor.

The creature howled in pain and fury before turning on Neuland. He grabbed the bottle of gasoline, and when the creature lunged at him with what was left of its mouth, he shoved the bottle inside, pulled one of his pistols, and shot it. The creature lurched backward, flames spouting from its mouth. As it fell onto its back in pain, Neuland picked up the duffel bag, then he and Tilda grabbed Ford and dragged him outside. They could still hear the creature bellowing when they reached the car.

They set Ford on the driveway and Neuland used a knife to cut away the portion of the creature's mouth still clinging to the man's arm.

"Oh my god," said Tilda when she saw the shredded skin and exposed wrist bone.

Neuland took a bottle and poured the contents over Ford's bleeding arm.

"What's that?" said Tilda.

"Holy water," said Neuland as he grabbed another bottle. "Now hydrogen peroxide to clean it."

As the peroxide began to foam in his wounds, Ford came to and groaned in pain. "Fuck," he rasped. He tried to sit up, but fell back, holding onto his bleeding arm.

"We have to get him back to Mansfield's," said Neuland. "I have painkillers and medical gear there."

He and Tilda piled Ford into the back of the Rolls, and they shot down the driveway away from Pale House.

At the mansion, Neuland kicked open the front door. He carried Ford inside and set him on the floor. Tilda grabbed a pillow from a sofa and put it behind his head.

Mansfield rolled up to them in his wheelchair. "What is this shit? Is the thing dead or not?" When no one answered, he shouted again, "Goddam you all, is it dead?"

"Ford is hurt," shouted Tilda. "We have to help him."

"So, you failed again," said the old man.

"Didn't you feel the quake?"

"What about it? That's no excuse."

"It wasn't their fault. They almost sent it away."

Mansfield scowled at her. "Bastards. I said kill the devil, not send it away. I need it."

"Why?"

Neuland stood up and said, "I don't know what you're yammering about, but I'm going upstairs for medical supplies. You stay away from him while I'm gone."

"Fuck you, dirt-napper," said Mansfield. He pulled a CO_2 gun from under the blanket on his lap and shot Neuland in the neck. He collapsed onto his back at the foot of Mansfield's chair.

"Mr. Mansfield," Tilda yelled.

"Shut up or you'll get a dart too." He rolled his wheelchair over to where Ford lay and looked him over. Satisfied with what he saw, he said, "To answer your earlier stupid question, I want the devil dead for one simple reason. I'm going to eat it."

"This is insane."

Mansfield rolled back to where Neuland lay. He said, "I won't eat all of it, of course. Just enough to gain its strength."

"For what?"

He looked at her and laughed. "Life. Immortality. I'm not going to die like this. I'm going to be reborn, fit and strong again."

"That was your plan this whole time?"

"Of course, you witless bitch. You're as useless as your mother."

Tilda's fear bled into a dark anger. "Don't talk about her like that."

She took a few steps toward Mansfield and he pointed the gun at her. She stopped.

"Sit down and don't move, or you'll be as dead as May."

Tilda dropped onto the sofa, tears forming in her eyes. "Oh god. Mom is dead? What happened?"

Mansfield ignored the question. He said, "If these two weren't so useless, I would have eaten as much of the devil as I could hold. Then, all I'd need is human flesh to live as long as I wanted." He looked at Tilda. "Yours to start with, but I guess we'll be going to Plan B. Eating this dead man's heart will accomplish much the same as eating the devil. Then I'll dine on young Ford. Be good and I'll let you watch."

He took a butcher knife from under his smoking jacket and plunged it into Neuland's chest.

17

Neuland was paralyzed. He drifted, half awake and half dreaming. Soon, his mind went very far away to the Deep South. Close to Easter, the time of resurrection. But Neuland had been resurrected years earlier, and was still working off his debt to the swamp witches and sorcerers who'd brought him back.

There had been a plague upon the land. The All-Consuming Eye had returned and was laying waste to the population. The eye's true name was Set-Taq Jihanuut, but even most magic folk were afraid to utter it. The Eye—immortal and unstoppable— had returned to the surface world after being banished to the deepest bowels of the earth so long ago that no one remembered how to replicate the spell that freed them from it.

Some of the local elders went far into the hills with offerings and pleas, and after twenty days, returned to the swamp with the forest hag known as Madame Pompidou. She was so old and had lived among the slash pines for so long that she resembled a tree herself. Her dry skin was like the bark of a black mangrove and her hair was strung like Spanish moss. Madame Pompidou brought something with her from the forest and presented it to the elders. They accepted it with a great deal of anxiety, because they knew what was in the sealed bark box and were afraid.

Madame Pompidou told them to bring smoked gator meat and the largest, meanest hogs in the territory. A day later, when the hogs arrived, people could scarcely believe their eyes. The beasts were twice as tall as any man and just as wide. And they were ravenous.

Once the hogs had been penned, Madame Pompidou told the elders to take what was in the bark box and put it with the gator meat. None of the men or women wanted to touch the box, much less open it. So, Neuland was called to the task. Madame Pompidou explained that all he had to do was upend the container within a foot of the smoked gator, and what was inside would do the rest.

Neuland went to the meat, shook out the contents of the box, and ran. He hid back among the trees and watched the rest from there. What had fallen from the box was a tangle of something that at first looked like long strands of yarn, wire, or drawings of nerve bundles he'd seen in schoolbooks. Yes, nerve bundles, but with a snake-like mouth and tongue at the end of each strand. They wormed their way hungrily into the gator meat until they disappeared. The moment they were out of sight, Madame Pompidou had the people release the hogs. The beasts charged the pile of meat and devoured it in less than a minute.

That night, the hogs were staked out at the edge of the water for Set-Taq Jihanuut. It didn't take the All-Consuming Eye long to smell the creatures. When the moon was high in the sky, it rose up from out of the swamp—the great round mouth in its iris open wide—and it swallowed each hog in a single bite. Madame Pompidou laughed and laughed because she knew the Eye had welcomed its death.

Inside Set-Taq Jihanuut, the hogs that had eaten the gator meat began to transform into something even larger and even hungrier. The bristles on their backs and sides turned to the sharpest steel. Their teeth grew into foot-long tusks, while their hooves burned like coals. Set-Taq Jihanuut, the All-Consuming Eye, wailed and thrashed in the filthy swamp water as the hogs began to eat it from the inside. It took an hour for the Eye to be reduced to a few shreds of stringy flesh, which the hogs fought over until there was not one iota of Set-Taq Jihanuut left.

Local hunters killed the mighty hogs with poisoned arrows, burned their bodies, and scattered their ashes in a nearby river where the current would take them safely out to sea.

In all the decades he'd been an indebted servant, and in all the years he'd been free to roam the world, Neuland never saw anything anywhere near as strange as that night in the swamp.

When the dream of Set-Taq Jihanuut ended, he felt the walls of death closing in on him again as they had so many years ago.

18

Mansfield managed to get the knife into Neuland's chest, but sitting in the chair made for an awkward angle when he tried sawing his way through to the dead man's heart. He had to lean over so far that his chest was almost touching his knees. He cursed and sweated, and finally gave up. When he shouted, "Tilda! Get over here and help me," she was already behind him with a small bronze replica of Rodin's Thinker she'd taken off the coffee table. She swung the sculpture at Mansfield's head. He realized what was happening at just the last minute and managed to dodge the full blow, but still caught the edge of The Thinker on the side of the head. He slid out of his chair, unconscious.

Tilda pulled the knife from Neuland's chest and threw it away. Fortunately, the old man was weak and hadn't been able to do too much damage. Still, Tilda was frightened and didn't know what to do. But she remembered there was a medical kit in Neuland's room. She ran upstairs and brought it back down just as Ford was coming to.

He looked around the room blearily. "What the fuck is going on?"

Tilda rushed to him with the medical kit. "Mr. Mansfield tried to cut out Neuland's heart. What do I do?"

Ford stared at her for a moment. Then said, "Where's Mansfield?"

"Over there. I hit him. He might be dead."

"Good. Help me to Neuland."

With Tilda under one arm, Ford was able to get up and shuffle to where his partner lay on the floor. "My arm is shit," he said. "You're going to have to do what I tell you."

"What do I do?"

"First, get that damn dart out of his neck. Then get the red bottle from the kit and pour some over Neuland's chest where the knife went in."

Tilda did as he said, pouring a generous amount of red liquid over Neuland's wound. It flowed thick like honey, but burned her eyes like cayenne pepper.

Ford said, "Now pack the wound with gauze and use the white medical tape to secure it in place."

She did as she was told and said, "Now what?"

"There's an autoinjector in the case. Open it and jam it into his neck where the dart went in."

"Okay," said Tilda. Then, "I did it. What else?"

"Slap him."

"What?"

"Slap the shit out of him. I'd do it, but I'm half lunch meat over here."

"I'm sorry," she said and slapped Neuland across the face.

"Harder. You're not Winnie the Pooh. Fucking let him have it."

Tilda hit him again.

"Better, but when I say 'three,' I want you to knock him to the goddamn moon. Ready?"

"No."

"One. Two. Three."

Tilda pulled back her arm and slapped Neuland as hard as she could. The concussion stung her hand and left it numb. She waited a moment, and just as she was about to hit Neuland again, he opened his eyes. Tilda grabbed him and helped him into a sitting position. He looked down at his chest.

"What the hell is this?" he said.

"Mr. Mansfield," said Tilda. "He was going to eat your heart."

"Really? The ballsy little shit," said Neuland, still dizzy. He looked around at Ford. "Are you all right?"

"My arm hurts like hell. I could use a little something for it. And a sling."

Tilda gave Neuland the medical kit. He found a bottle of Norco and gave his partner two pills. Ford dry swallowed them and made a face at the bitterness.

There was a hat rack by the door. Tilda took one of Mansfield's silk scarves off it, fashioned it into a sling, and slipped it over Ford's head. He flexed his shoulders and said, "Thanks, that's a lot better."

Neuland crawled over and checked Mansfield's pulse. "The old monster is still alive. Now, what was that about him eating my heart?"

"He said it would make him immortal. That's why he wanted the devil. It would do the same, but we couldn't kill it, so he settled for you."

"Settled," said Ford, and laughed. "Second place to a walking piece of shit. That has to hurt."

"It does a little," said Neuland.

Tilda dropped down onto the sofa. "He also said that Mom was dead. He knew it this whole time."

Neuland went and sat next to Tilda. "She left soon after the devil arrived, didn't she?"

Tilda nodded. "Yeah. She did."

"And your father hung himself soon after that."

"What's your point?"

"Because of what happened at the house, and because of a dream I just had," said Neuland. "Mansfield didn't like your mother much after she married, did he?"

"Not at all. He could be very cruel."

"What are you thinking?" said Ford, getting up and sitting in a love seat across from them.

Neuland said, "I think Mansfield raised the creature, but couldn't control it. He tried to kill it, but like us, he needed bait."

Tilda put a hand to her mouth. "No. He wouldn't. Oh god, Mom."

"I think your father found out and that's why he killed himself."

"Fuck me," said Ford. "Let's just shoot him and get out of here."

"No," said Neuland. "He wanted the devil. Maybe he can help us get rid of it once and for all."

"You want to go back there?"

"Of course. That thing killed Tilda's mother." Neuland got up and kicked Mansfield. "And this asshole is responsible for her father's death."

Ford adjusted his sling and said, "So what's the plan? Our weapons didn't do shit and we lost most of our gear in the quake."

"We're not going to use weapons this time. And we're not going to use any rituals."

"Then what?" said Tilda.

"We're going to slip it a Mickey," said Neuland. "But we're going to need new bait. I know who I choose."

Ford said, "Me too." He looked at Tilda. "What about you?"

Tilda was crying quietly, but caught her breath and said, "Mr. Mansfield killed my parents. Fed Mom to the devil. He should feel what that's like."

"Good," said Neuland. "Let me grab a few things and we can get back to Pale House before dark."

19

When they reached the house, they piled Mansfield out of the back seat, propped him in his wheelchair, and carried them both up onto the front porch.

"What now?" said Tilda.

Neuland took a jar from his pocket and showed it to her. She recognized it immediately when she saw all the eyes staring back at her.

"What's that for?" she said.

"We're going to feed them to him," Neuland said.

"What are they?"

"*Ganrooks.* Insects. The burrowing kind. Carnivorous. They'll eat anything. You still want to be here for this?"

Tilda nodded. "I have to be."

"Seeing how Ford is useless at the moment..."

"Thank you," Ford said.

"You're welcome." To Tilda, Neuland said, "You're going to have to hold back his head while I pour these down his gullet."

"Do I have to look?"

"No. Just keep his head back so his mouth stays open and his throat is straight."

"I can do that."

"Then do it now."

Tilda pulled Mansfield's head back as far as she could and held it there. Neuland took a narrow length of clear plastic tubing from his back pocket and slowly slid it down Mansfield's throat. The old man sputtered and coughed, but Neuland kept feeding the tube down into his stomach. When there were only a few inches of tubing left, he stopped and took the top off the bottle of insects. Before he could pour them into the tube, Ford said, "Hold on. You're not leaving me out this. Let me do it."

Neuland stepped aside and held the tube as Ford carefully poured the contents of the jar down the open end. When the bottle was empty, he threw it away and Neuland withdrew the tube.

"You can let go now," Ford told Tilda.

She released Mansfield and took a step back. "Is it done?"

"It went just fine."

"Now what?"

Neuland took a thumb-size snap pack of smelling salts from his breast pocket. "I think he should be awake for this. Don't you?"

"Absolutely."

Neuland started to do it, but Tilda took the pack from his hand and broke it under Mansfield's nose. The old man sputtered and cried out, trying to bat Tilda's hands away. Finally, he was awake. He looked around at the three of them and then at Pale House.

"What are you pimps up to? Tilda, take me back home."

"We're at your home, Papa Shep. The one where you killed Mom."

"What?" he said, his voice growing soft. "No, child. You misunderstood me. Whatever these men told you are lies."

"You're the liar. The way you've been lying to me my whole life. But that was your last lie. I hope you enjoyed it."

Mansfield's face hardened again. "What's the plan then, you bastards? You going to cast another brilliant spell and you need me to hold your dicks out of the way while you fail again?"

"No," said Ford. "We're waiting for you."

"For what?"

Neuland said, "You'll know it when it happens."

Mansfield looked around again and pushed the forward control on his wheelchair. Nothing happened.

"Don't bother," said Tilda. "We cut the wires to the battery."

"With the knife you used on me," said Neuland.

Mansfield looked at Pale House nervously and held up his hands. "Okay. You win. Do you know how much I'm worth? What this family is worth? Tilda's trust fund alone would make you rich men. But I'll sign over everything. Every dollar. Every bit of real estate. Just get me away from this shithole."

Ford turned to Tilda. "He's trying to sell you out. Again."

Neuland said, "What do you want to do, Tilda? Do we let him go?"

"Sure," she said. She bent over to Mansfield and said, "If you can roll your chair back to the other house all by yourself, we will one-hundred-percent let you go."

Mansfield looked from her to the men and grabbed the wheels of his wheelchair. But they didn't budge. He twisted around and tried to reach back to the battery. "The levers," he said. "The freewheel levers. I can't reach them."

"These little yellow things back here? Yeah, you're never going to get to them in time," said Ford.

"In time for what? What have you done, you pricks?" He made a face and doubled over as his stomach cramped. "Did you bastards drug me?"

Tilda said, "You should be so lucky. You made everyone around you suffer. Now you get to know how that feels."

Mansfield clutched his stomach. "Tilda, I only did what was right for the family."

"More lies." She looked at the men. "What do we do now?"

"It's simple really," said Neuland. "See, we can't kill the devil, but we can obliterate it."

"You're going to let those little *ganrooks* eat it, aren't you?" said Tilda.

"Yes. After they eat Mansfield. All we have to do is take him inside and wait for the devil."

"Let me do it," said Tilda. "This is family business."

Neuland flipped the freewheel levers and Tilda rolled Mansfield inside Pale House, all the way to the remains of the salt circle. Mansfield grabbed her hand. "Tilda. Please."

She snatched it away. "You brought the devil to our family. You can send it away."

Mansfield slumped over in his chair, holding his stomach and moaning. A thick line of blood trickled from his mouth onto his lap. Tilda stood there for a moment as if she might change her mind.

From the door Ford called, "What are you waiting for? Get out of there."

She said, "How do we know the devil will find him before the bugs eat him? Shouldn't we call it?"

"He's the head of the family. It will find him."

Tilda shook her head. "No. I have to see it. I have to know." She raised a foot and brought it down hard on the floor. She did it again and yelled, "We're here. Can you hear us, devil? Come and eat us."

Something rumbled downstairs.

"Tilda," yelled Neuland.

The rumbling moved, crashing through timbers and knocking obstructions from its path. Tilda kept stamping on the floor.

"We're here!" she yelled.

Something creaked, and the damaged floorboard she'd been stamping on snapped in two. Her leg fell through, pinning her.

At the other end of the house, something was battering its way up the half-collapsed stairs. Tilda struggled to pull her leg out, but only succeeded in ripping into her flesh.

Mansfield was screaming in his chair. Even in his agony, when he saw Tilda he laughed. "You're as useless as them."

Ford and Neuland ran into the parlor just as the creature—its protruding mouth blistered, but almost fully regrown—rushed them, knocking timbers and splintered furniture from its path.

Neuland bent to Tilda and kicked away the boards that had trapped her leg. She pounded at the boards with her fists as they began to give.

Ford ran past her and grabbed Mansfield's chair with his one good arm. The old man reached back and tried to stop him, then cried out in pain as insects boiled out of his abdomen. Ford ran, pushing Mansfield before him right at the charging devil.

The creature roared in triumph and Mansfield screamed as it swallowed him whole. While it choked down the chair, Ford ran back to where Neuland had Tilda out of the floor. The boards had gouged her leg badly, but they got on each side of her and half-walked, half-dragged her outside.

They made it to the Rolls-Royce and fell back against it. Inside Pale House, the devil continued to thrash and roar. The old building swayed a little as it battered the walls in pain.

"How long will it take?" said Tilda.

"Not long," Neuland replied. "We'll know when it gets quiet."

"So, the bugs eat the devil. But what happens to the bugs?"

He took a lighter from his pocket. "Then we kill the bugs."

Tilda grabbed it from him. "Mr. Mansfield is gone. It's my house now. Let me do it."

They waited by the car. Tilda had the front door of the Rolls open and was sitting in the passenger seat, listening with the others as the creature smashed Pale House to pieces. The whole house rocked back and forth. One of the tall turrets crashed to the ground. Then the roof collapsed, bringing the walls down with it. The sound was deafening, but for a moment they could hear the devil wailing over the din. When the sound of cracking wood ended, there was just silence, from the house and the creature.

Without a word, Tilda got out of the car and limped to the rubble. She held the lighter to some curtains until they caught. She went from place to place around the house, igniting small timbers like kindling. Soon, some of the small fires caught enough of the large beams and wooden walls' slats that the whole building began to burn.

The three of them watched until the sun got low in the sky. Then Neuland got into the driver's seat and drove them back to what, until very recently, had been Mr. Mansfield's concrete fortress.

20

B ack at the house, Neuland patched up Tilda and gave her one of Mansfield's canes to get around on until her leg healed. Then he found Ford a better sling from the medical kit. After that, the three of them collapsed on sofas in the parlor, exhausted. An hour or so passed, then Neuland said, "Can I make a suggestion?"

"Of course," said Tilda.

"Don't ever go into the chapel. In fact, burn it like Pale House."

She frowned. "Why? What's in it?"

"You know all the stuff you saw today?" said Ford.

"Yes?"

"The chapel is worse."

"I'll burn it. But not right this minute. I'm just want to sit here until Christmas."

"I guess you're a rich woman now," said Neuland.

"I guess. But all I feel is numb."

"I understand. But in a few days it will start fade, and in a few weeks you'll feel like yourself again."

Ford said, "You can lock this place up and do anything you want. Go anywhere you want."

Tilda sat up a little straighter. "Wow. You're right. I'm free. Free *and* rich. What a strange feeling. Oh. That reminds me." Tilda limped on the cane to a wall safe and brought back an impressive stack of money. "Four hundred thousand for killing the devil."

They left the money on the table and Neuland said, "Thank you. That makes up for a lot of wear and tear."

She said, "What are you two going to do now?"

Ford leaned back and looked up at the ceiling. "When we first got to California, we thought we might stay a while."

"But after this, California can kiss our asses goodbye," said Neuland.

Tilda said, "Where does that leave you?"

"We talked it over last night," said Ford. "We decided that if we made it through this alive, fuck it. We're going back to New York."

Tilda brightened. "Great. I'll get us a private jet."

"Us?"

Neuland said, "When did *us* happen?"

Tilda made a face at them. "Look at you two. You only have one arm, and you have a hole in your chest. Honestly, I don't know how you've survived this long without someone like me."

Ford adjusted his sling and said, "You handled that shotgun pretty well."

"And you didn't run when you could have," said Neuland.

She ticked off a list on her fingers. "Plus, I can keep books, run an office, and I'm a whiz with computers."

"Those are all things we're not whizzes at."

Ford said, "Actually, we don't do them at all."

Neuland looked at him. "Maybe we could try things the smart way and not find out we're broke and end up scrambling for money all the time."

"So," said Tilda. "Am I in the gang?"

"Yes, but..."

Ford said, "On a trial basis."

Tilda limped over and hugged them both.

"Do you want to pack some things?" said Neuland.

She laughed. "Are you kidding? I packed a bag when this whole thing started. I was leaving no matter what."

"I promised you a steak dinner in town," said Ford. He looked at Neuland. "You okay for goofer juice?"

"I have plenty."

Tilda sat back and said, "Thank you for this. For everything."

"Don't thank us yet. There are people in New York we have to make nice with.

If we survive that, then you can thank us."

Tilda got up and went to a desk across the room. "I'll arrange for our flight."

Once she'd left, Ford said, "Is this really a good idea?"

"Do you have any better ones?" said Neuland. "We can't leave her here. She's a good kid."

"I know. That's what worries me. You saw what she did today. What if she's better at our jobs than we are?"

"Then I guess she'll be the boss."

"Look at her," Ford said. "You think she'll dump us eventually and go out on her own?"

"Definitely. She's young and she'll get tired of us telling her the same boring stories over and over."

"I guess you're right. We'll have to let our little bird fly."

"But until then..." said Ford.

"Until then it will be fun having someone new around."

"Oh no. Are we fathers now?"

"Uncles at best. And don't ever say that to her or me again."

Tilda came back a few minutes later. "We're set. We leave tomorrow at noon from SFO. I even got us booked into a nice hotel in Manhattan. If that's all right."

"That's more than all right," said Neuland.

"Which car should we take to town?" said Tilda.

Ford said, "Not the Rolls."

Neuland said, "Absolutely not the Rolls."

Tilda said, "Let's go outside and figure it out."

They all went out together and Tilda locked the fortress behind them.

They took the red Cadillac convertible, and after a night on the town in San Francisco, they abandoned it at the airport.

ACKNOWLEDGEMENTS

I'd like to thank my wonderful agent, Ginger Clark, who's stuck with me through so many ups and downs, and found the book a home. I also want to thank my terrific editor, George Sandison, who made *The Pale House Devil* much more than I ever thought it could be. I also want to thank Cassandra Khaw, who pointed me in the right direction when the book seemed like it was going to sink into the sea. And, of course, Aces, who sleeps by my desk and eats my Post-Its whenever I turn my back.

ABOUT THE AUTHOR

Richard Kadrey is the *New York Times*-bestselling author of the Sandman Slim supernatural noir series. *Sandman Slim* was included in Amazon's "100 Science Fiction & Fantasy Books to Read in a Lifetime," and is in development as a feature film. Some of Kadrey's other books include *King Bullet, The Grand Dark, Butcher Bird,* and *The Dead Take the A Train* (with Cassandra Khaw). He's written for film and comics, including Heavy Metal, Lucifer, and Hellblazer. Kadrey also makes music with his band, A Demon in Fun City.

ALSO AVAILABLE FROM TITAN BOOKS

THE DEAD TAKE THE A TRAIN

by Richard Kadrey and Cassandra Khaw

A gritty, explosive and bloody cosmic horror about a roguish magical fixer, who is the only thing stopping the finance industry from summoning the eldritch beings they worship and serve.

Julie Crews is a coked-up, burnt-out thirty-something who packs a lot of magic into her small body. She's trying to establish herself as a major Psychic Operative in the NYC magic scene, and she'll work the most gruesome gigs to claw her way to the top.

Desperate to break the dead-end grind, Julie summons a guardian angel for a quick career boost. But when her power grab accidentally releases an elder god hellbent on the annihilation of our galaxy, the body count rises rapidly.

The *Dead Take the A Train* is a high-octane cocktail of Khaw's cosmic horror and Kadrey's gritty fantasy—shaken, not stirred.

TITANBOOKS.COM

ALSO AVAILABLE FROM TITAN BOOKS

NOTHING BUT BLACKENED TEETH

by Cassandra Khaw

Cat joins her old friends, who are in search of the perfect wedding venue, to spend the night in a Heian-era manor in Japan. Trapped in webs of love, responsibility and yesterdays, they walk into a haunted house with their hearts full of ghosts.

This mansion is long abandoned, but it is hungry for new guests, and welcomes them all—welcomes the demons inside them—because it is built on foundations of sacrifice and bone.

Their night of food, drinks, and games quickly spirals into a nightmare as the house draws them into its embrace. For lurking in the shadows is the ghost bride with a black smile and a hungry heart.

And she gets lonely down there in the dirt.

"Brutally delicious! Khaw is a master of teasing your senses, and then terrorizing them!"

N.K. Jemisin, *New York Times* bestselling
author of *The Fifth Season*

TITANBOOKS.COM

ALSO AVAILABLE FROM TITAN BOOKS

SISTER, MAIDEN, MONSTER

by Lucy A. Snyder

Humanity has been irrevocably changed by a virus that radically alters its victims… yet life goes on.

Three women must band together to try to survive. Erin and Savannah are helping usher in the new world, while Mareva has been burdened with a very special task—one she's too horrified to even acknowledge.

A beautifully written, cosmically horrifying, wholly unique story that examines the roots of our belief systems and completely defies all expectations.

"Lucy A. Snyder has always been a trailblazer, and with *Sister, Maiden, Monster,* she scorches the earth with the sheer audacity of her imagination. A hideously gory, kink-fueled, feminist cosmic horror apocalypse novel that should be on the top of everyone's reading list."

Christopher Golden, *New York Times* bestselling author of *Ararat* and *Road of Bones*

TITANBOOKS.COM

For more fantastic fiction, author events,
exclusive excerpts, competitions, limited editions and more

VISIT OUR WEBSITE
titanbooks.com

LIKE US ON FACEBOOK
facebook.com/titanbooks

FOLLOW US ON TWITTER AND INSTAGRAM
@TitanBooks

EMAIL US
readerfeedback@titanemail.com